Hailing from Galway, Frank Fahy has had a varied career as a teacher, journalist, publisher, and musician. The one common denominator in his life is the presence of books.

As an award-winning writer and lyricist, he has been recognised at the SiarScéal International Literary Festival for his captivating short story, *Western Medley Surprise.* In 2019, Frank published his debut poetry collection, *Building New Bridges,* showcasing his prowess as a poet.

Frank's enduring passion for literature led him to co-found the Write-on group, where he collaborates with fellow members to edit and publish an annual anthology. His unwavering love for the written word continues to inspire and enrich his creative journey.

by the same author

Building New Bridges – A Collection of Poems

A Father's Love

and Other Stories

FRANK FAHY

First Published 2023
Frank Fahy Publishing Services,
5 Village Centre, Barna, Galway,
Ireland.

Cover photograph: *Screebe Fisherman's Hut*,
Connemara, Galway © Professor Chaosheng Zhang,
University of Galway, 2023. All rights reserved.

Paperback Edition ISBN: 9798392432745
Imprint: Independently published by
Frank Fahy Publishing Services, Barna, Galway,
Ireland.

**Comhairle Chontae na Gaillimhe
Galway County Council**

Dedication

To the cherished members of our Write-on Group, whose attentive ears and thoughtful insights breathed life into the early drafts of these stories, your invaluable input shaped the final form of this collection;

To the exceptional Mary Rose Tobin, whose expertise in proofreading and unwavering support transformed the dream of this collection into reality;

And to my beloved mother, now watching from beyond, who planted the seeds of a lifelong passion for writing and nurtured my creativity from its earliest days;

This book is dedicated to each of you, with heartfelt appreciation and love.

Contents

A Father's Love

From New Jersey, was it?' the matron inquired, a glimmer of curiosity in her eyes as they settled on Patrick.

'Yes, New Jersey,' Patrick affirmed.

The matron nodded thoughtfully. 'He used to speak of America, you know. He insisted he had family there. But as the years slipped away, and no word arrived, we thought that perhaps he was mistaken. It's not uncommon for people to mix up what they see on television screens with the real world.'

Patrick's heart sank like a stone in still waters. His grandfather, Joseph O'Flaherty, was cast adrift, and left to languish in this nursing home on the rain-soaked coast of Ireland.

The matron, a solid and formidable woman, arched a single eyebrow at Patrick, as if to gauge whether he had accepted her explanation. But the young man, his focus sharpened by his mission, barely acknowledged her scrutiny. Instead, he surveyed the space around him, taking in the fragrance of lavender from the carpet, the soft hum of the modern computer, and the orderly array of papers and books.

'The family lost touch, ma'am,' Patrick admitted.

'He never mentioned family,' she said. 'He had a son?'

Patrick's brow furrowed. 'His son's name was Jack, ma'am. I'm Jack's boy, Patrick.'

Recognition blossomed in the matron's eyes. 'Ah, I see,' she murmured softly. 'You're Joseph O'Flaherty's grandson.'

'Yes, ma'am. My dad passed in February of this year,' Patrick said, his voice laden with emotion.

'I'm so sorry...' the matron offered, her words trailing off into the air.

'He was only forty-seven years old. My mom, Rosetta, is devastated. We're all heartbroken,' Patrick confided, his eyes welling with tears.

As he spoke, the memory of his mother rose in his mind. She had been a bastion of strength during his father's funeral, but Patrick knew that beneath her composed exterior, she was in pieces.

He did all he could to assist at the wake, determined to be a pillar for his mother. She had tasked him with serving drinks to the mourners, and he moved among the Italians with wine and beer, and among the Irish with whiskey and Guinness. While pouring drinks for three of his father's workmen, Patrick overheard a fragment of their conversation that stirred his curiosity.

Larry O'Sullivan spoke in a hushed tone, saying, 'No family made the journey across,' to which his companion replied, 'All gone by now, I suppose.'

'I don't think so,' Larry responded. 'I've a feeling his father is still alive. Too old to travel, I suppose. No great loss.'

Jack's father? Patrick was taken aback by this revelation, for he had never heard of any Irish relations before. He longed to confront the men and demand answers, but he remembered his father's counsel to bide his time and listen attentively.

Patrick eventually joined the men, and as he replenished their glasses with generous pours of Jameson, he listened with rapt attention to their tales of work on construction sites, men hired and fired, scaffolding and cranes that toppled in fierce winds, and accidents narrowly averted. He was heartened to hear of his father's wisdom and the high regard in which these men held him, but he was also vigilant for any snippets of information about Ireland that could help him unlock the secrets of his family.

As the night wore on and the mourners departed, Patrick assisted his mother in tidying away the dishes and glasses. In his mind, he also tidied the scraps of information he had gathered, which would help him begin his search.

In the fading afternoon light, the nursing home building in Galway cast a gentle, melancholic glow over the lush Irish landscape.

'Harvard, did you say?' the matron inquired, her voice a blend of scepticism and curiosity. 'Harvard, no less.'

'No, ma'am. William Paterson University, New Jersey. My tutor advised me to use my vacation wisely. 'Go to Ireland,' he said. 'Catch up on your past before it's too late. Stones don't talk; only people do!"

'Wise counsel, and I'm delighted that you've come this far. Remember, though... your grandad gets very mixed up. You'll need to be cautious figuring out what's true and what's not.'

'All I can do is try, ma'am.'

Together with the matron, Patrick made his way to his grandfather's private room, which was bright and homely, equipped with a nurse call system, a telephone, and a TV set. The room had a sparkling clean feel and smelled fresh. In the evanescent light of that late April afternoon, the old, wizened man in a cotton pyjama top, resting against a mountain of pillows, seemed oddly out of place. His face was creased and lined. His hollow eyes were bloodshot. His tongue worried his gums and saliva dripped from his mouth. The matron took a damp facecloth from the ensuite bathroom and wiped the old man's face clean. 'Sit up now, Joe,' she said kindly. 'You have a visitor.'

'A visitor,' he mumbled. 'For me?'

'Hello, Mr O'Flaherty,' said the young man cheerfully. 'I'm Patrick. Your grandson.'

The old man's watery eyes widened. 'Grandson?'

'Yes, sir! I'm Jack's boy.'

'Sit me up, sonny,' the old man muttered. 'Sit me up 'til I've a look at you. Jack's boy, you say?'

'Yes. I'm Patrick.'

The matron interrupted. 'You told me before that you had family in America,' she said. 'Well, here's your flesh and blood. He's come to talk with you. Maybe you'd be up to answering a few of his questions?'

'What d'you want to know?' the old man grumbled.

'Oh... nothing much, Grandpa. I'm on a gap year in Europe and I thought now was a great time to find out more about my family.'

'Your family, is it?'

The matron coughed politely and said that she would get a nurse to bring them both a cup of tea. 'We'll open the French windows here so that you can sit together and talk for a while.'

A gentle sea breeze flooded the room. The matron made her exit quietly, leaving the two men to get acquainted.

'This really is a beautiful place, Grandpa,' Patrick said as he looked out the window.

'D'ya hear the gulls?' the old man inquired.

'Yes, Grandpa.'

'Seagulls in my ears. All my life.' He coughed.

Patrick turned back towards the bed and helped to raise the old man higher on his pillows. It felt as if he was lifting a skeleton. Joe's chest rose and fell in rasping staccatos; the stench of stale breath accompanied every wheeze. His eyes drifted as he searched his memory banks. When he spoke again, it was as if he was talking to himself.

'Put on the kettle. Put the kettle on the boil.'

'The nurse will be here with the tea shortly,' said Patrick.

'How is he? How is Jack?'

'Oh. I'm sorry, Grandpa. I didn't realise. Did they not tell you?'

'Tell me?' said Joe.

'My dad died last spring.'

Silence filled the empty space between them. For a while, neither man spoke.

'Last spring,' the old man whispered. His eyes darted from side to side. 'Spring. The Thyestes Chase.'

'The Thyestes Chase?' Patrick said.

'Yes! Biggest race on the calendar in springtime.'

'I don't understand, Grandpa. A race?'

'She was in hospital, you see! In hospital. Her back.'

'Who are you talking about, Grandpa?'

'Jack's mother, Eileen. My wife!'

'Gran,' whispered Patrick.

'We were rushing back from the hospital. We got her from the car onto the wheelchair. Over to the front door. Twenty minutes to three o'clock. Just twenty minutes to the start of the race.'

'You and my dad brought Gran home from hospital?'

Joe continued as though he had not heard.

'At the bottom of the stairs, I said to Jack: 'You go to the kitchen and put on the kettle, son. I'll take her from here.'

Put on the kettle. Put the kettle on the boil. Is that what he was talking about earlier?

'I managed to get Eileen up the stairs and into bed. I propped her head with pillows. She was in a lot of pain. But she had tablets.'

'And what happened?' Patrick asked in a hushed whisper, afraid to interrupt the old man's train of thought.

'I told her that Jack had the kettle boiled, and that I'd bring her up a cup of tea. She said that she'd love a cup of tea. I ran down the stairs into the kitchen. Jack was gone. Blast it! The kettle was empty.'

Joe took a fit of coughing.

'So, Dad didn't fill the kettle. What did it matter, Grandpa?'

Ignoring Patrick's comment, the old man twisted and turned in the bed. His agitation increased. He wheezed and coughed repeatedly. The more he tried to raise his voice, the weaker he became.

'Take it easy, Grandpa. Take it easy. I can come back another time. Why don't you get some rest?'

But Joe was determined to finish what he had started.

'I shouted up the stairs to Eileen that I had to go out for a minute. I'd bring up her tea later. On the way out the door I kicked the wheelchair out of my way. It was ten minutes to three.'

'So, Granny was left on her own at home,' Patrick muttered. 'You and my dad left her there?'

'Aye! Aye! It was race day, you see. The Thyestes. Our horse was running.'

'And you didn't even bring her up the cup of tea?'

'The kettle wasn't boiled. The last thing I said to him was... was...' He sat up in the bed. 'Why didn't he do it? Oh, Jack, Jack... if only you had done as I asked...' He stared out the window with a vacant gaze.

A cloud had eclipsed the sun, and specks of rain began to drizzle, some of them dampening the floor inside the French windows. Patrick rose and closed the windows. He was hesitant to speak. Before his arrival, he had not known what to expect. The tale he was listening to now stirred an uneasy sensation in the pit of his stomach. He contemplated fleeing the room, but he sensed that this was his sole chance to hear the truth. To discover what had transpired between a father and a son so many years ago... long before he was born.

'The official distance was...' The old man had spoken again.

'What's that?' inquired Patrick as he hastened back to his grandfather's side.

'Lightning Bolt won by a neck,' the old man whispered.

'So, your horse won?' said Patrick, attempting to encourage the man in the bed to continue speaking.

'Jack and I wanted to roar and shout, but we were the only two winners in the bookies, teeming with irate punters. I squeezed my son's shoulders. 'You've no idea how much money I'm just after winning!' I whispered into his ear. Without a pause, Jack replied: 'You've no idea how much money I'm after winning."

'You both fared well. Your horse won. And you had it well backed,' said Patrick.

'At the time, I believed Jack meant the hundred pounds I'd given him, and I calculated that he now had six hundred towards his USA fund.'

Over the next few minutes, Patrick learned that his father, with Larry O'Sullivan, and some other pals had made a pact. They had decided to pool their money and to have a right good bet on Lightning Bolt. If the horse lost, they would stay in Ireland for the summer and travel to the USA the following year. If he won, they would have the time of their lives in America. Lightning Bolt bore the lives of Jack and his friends on his back.

The old man's voice grew weaker.

'He was a quiet one, was Jack. He didn't tell me then. It was much later when I found out. How could I chastise him for not boiling the kettle?'

Patrick felt that the old man had expended enough energy in the telling of his tale.

'Why don't you rest now, Grandpa?' he said gently.

Joe was determined to continue, his voice a quivering filament of sound, narrating the events.

'At the teller's counter, I collected seventy pounds from one of my smaller bets, leaving the larger stash to be sorted out over the next few days. O'Reilly's Bar was next door to the bookies. "Let's go for a drink,' I said to Jack.

The memory of the celebrations brought a smile to the old man's face. Patrick could picture the scenes as the story unfurled. The two men buying drinks for everyone, toasts being raised, and songs sung. Those who hadn't backed the winner quickly cheering up and joining in. The crowded bar filling with whoops of joy and cries of laughter. His father keeping the barman occupied and the party going. Grandpa and dad slapping each other on the back – the greatest punters of all time. They had money, they had friends, they had porter, they had each other.

'Gran, at home in bed, missed all the excitement?' mused Patrick.

Silence.

'It was not that late when we returned, perhaps six o'clock,' the old man took up the story. 'I left the car outside the pub and we both ambled home. We relived the race time and again... how the favourite had led over the last, only to be surpassed by the fast-finishing Lightning Bolt. It was the most exquisite race. It was the most splendid day – a great day to be alive.'

A cloud blocked the sunlight causing the room to darken suddenly. Joe coughed and Patrick helped him to take a sip of water.

'I remember fumbling with the front door key,' he said. 'The lock yielded eventually. Something obstructed the door from inside. The wheelchair. I pressed against it, and it gradually gave way. Her crumpled form lay at the bottom of the stairs.'

'Gran?' said Patrick.

Joe closed his eyes and sighed lengthily. Patrick shuddered when he heard that the coroner's report called it Death by misadventure and went on to state that Grandma might have survived the tumble down the stairs, but her neck snapped when it struck the aluminium frame of the wheelchair.

'She fell down the stairs and broke her neck?' said Patrick. 'Oh, my God!'

The young man stood and paced about. 'What did my father do? What did you do?'

'What could we do?' the old man sobbed. 'My poor Eileen.'

He tried to elevate himself on his pillows as best he could. Patrick didn't come to his aid.

'I can't recall much else. Did I cradle her in my arms? Did we attempt to revive her? Who rang for the ambulance? When did the neighbours arrive? It's all a blur. I remember the funeral. Jack was there, dressed in a black suit. His friend, Larry O'Sullivan, and some others, helped bear the coffin. He stood with them the whole time. He maintained a distance from me.'

'Did you ever speak again?'

'No. Shortly after, I was informed that he had gone to the States. I guessed he had a student visa and thought he'd return. But I never heard from him, and I never tried to contact him.'

Patrick listened, his heart compressed taut within his chest.

Joe's recollections became more fragmented and disjointed, like broken glass reflecting splintered images of a life long vanished. Nothing had bridged the chasm that had widened between him and his son, and the unvoiced blame that had haunted them both.

'Did you blame him for what happened?' Patrick ventured, his voice soft, like a feather on the wind.

'Blame? What is blame? Two days earlier, if Eileen hadn't stood on the bed to change the lightbulb... If the mattress had been properly aligned... If she hadn't crashed into the bookshelves... If the doctors had released her from the hospital a few minutes earlier... If Jack had boiled the kettle... Who knows?' the old man mused, his voice heavy with unanswered questions.

Patrick felt his grandfather's words envelop him like a thick, woollen shroud. He could almost hear the whispers of a distant spring afternoon, filled with regrets. A race won, a life lost, and a family forever fractured.

As Joe's words began to blur and fade, a nurse entered the room, her arms laden with a tray bearing china cups and saucers, a matching teapot, and a plate of Custard Creams.

Patrick escaped to the corridor seeking refuge from the shadows of a long-hidden family secret. From inside he heard his grandfather say, 'I'd kill for a cup of tea.'

In the cold air, Patrick thought of the old man, confined by memories, and of his father, Jack, who fled Ireland to escape an unchangeable past. He considered his grandmother, Eileen, who had paid the ultimate price for a simple, unfulfilled request. He wondered if he would have acted differently in their shoes.

Patrick knew his grandfather's story would linger, even after the day had turned to twilight. And he would never look at a boiling kettle without recalling the sorrowful refrain that haunted his grandfather's final days:

You can pass the winning post a neck in front, but you still might not win.

My First Book

Perched on the delicate tips of my toes, I manipulated the spherical, yellowed handle of the timeworn kitchen door. As it yawned before me, tendrils of steam danced in the air, emanating from the colossal Aga. The saccharine allure of cinnamon. A symphony of apples. The sizzling serenade of succulent steak. Glossy tiles, ebony and ivory, bore the soft imprints of footfall, crisscrossing to and from the pantry like an ephemeral dance.

From the diaphanous haze, Mama emerged, taken aback. 'Jesus, Mary and Joseph, child! Don't come a step further!'

Sometimes when she prayed, she shouted.

'Mama, Mama, look! I write-ed a book!'

'Don't stand... Oh, heavenly mercy!'

Then, in a softer, kinder voice, 'Did you write something, pet?' Her paisley apron exhaled plumes of flour.

'Mama, look! Pages – full-ed!'

Mama's thoughts should have been occupied with the apple pie baking in the oven. Himself hates it when the crust gets too hard and brown, and the meat for the stew would be overcooked if she didn't turn it in the pan, and the carrots needed to be washed and sliced, and, – Lord and his Blessed Mother, – she forgot the parsnips, – himself always likes a few parsnips, and the potatoes needed peeling, and her curranty cake was only half ready, and the blessed flour had to be cleaned up from the floor, and ... and ...

Would you look at my little dote? – poor Francis, the copybook nearly as big as himself, (bless him!) and the scrawls all over the pages.

Sweet Jesus! but he didn't half use the crayon. Well, bless his little heart, the poor *manín* and the big blue eyes of him.

Would you look at the hole in his *geansaí*? Oooh Sacred Divine ... could you ever keep them in clothes?

'Mama, it's my book – my N-E-W book!'

Mama's hands clasped her head. Flecks of white streaked her beautiful brown hair. I gasped at the way she suddenly looked so old.

As I clung firmly to my precious manuscript, Mama swept me up into her arms. Gently prising the copybook from my fists, she settled me onto her knee.

'Now, little man, what have we got here?'

'I've been working hard, Mama, like you said, very, very hard, and, I've been writing, and writing, and writing, and I fulled up...

the WHOLE book....

And look, Mama, I stayed inside the lines and... I'll need a new book now.'

'Oh! A book? You have written a complete book? What a clever little man! Who is the best writer in the world? Myyyy little man! And in such a short time! Sacred Heart! Now! Will we read it?'

'Yes, Mama! You read it and I'll tell you if you're right.'

Exhausted after all my hard work, I snuggled up in her warm lap.

Cosy.

And I listened to her read.

And I helped her to turn the pages.

And I made sure that she didn't make any mistakes.

Jimmy Brady

On a radiant Saturday afternoon, a sense of mystery and expectancy pervaded our car as we covered the miles from Dublin to Bride's Cross. A turn to the right, where a signpost heralded Doonaree, just a few miles further on. The vestiges of the day's light grasped at the encroaching darkness above. Beyond the bridge across the river, the village emerged. We inched along the main thoroughfare, our gaze seeking the school. A charming grocery, a butcher's, a pair of churches, and four public houses graced our view—a quintessential rural Irish tableau, yet the school eluded us.

Having reached the football pitch at the village's edge, we doubled back, once more passing the shops, churches, and pubs. Tenacity prevented me from stopping to ask for directions. We pressed on to the outskirts, marvelling at the bucolic comfort. Doonaree, the Fort of the King, lay serene and somnolent.

Upon this side road, we saw a factory, a walled estate, and in an isolated field, the old schoolhouse – a single-storeyed, elongated building, encircled by a squat concrete barrier, its iron gates secured with padlocks. The main whitewashed building was surrounded by prefabricated, ramshackle, provisional classrooms. A pastoral panorama unfolded, with golden cornfields undulating in the tender summer breeze. It was a Saturday evening, the sinking sun cast its reflections upon the rectangular windows. We vaulted over the low wall and crossed into an enchanted, mystic realm.

Returning to the village square, we were greeted by a grand oak and the Parochial House. A shared, impulsive inspiration seized us, and we resolved to knock. The door creaked open, and furtive, rodent-like eyes peered out from a ruddy, rotund face.

'We're looking for the Parish Priest,' I said.

'Not here,' came the curt response.

The curate wearing a black tunic, and brown open-toed sandals appeared to be awakening from a slumber. Dreams unsettled; his expression clouded. Yet the evening was young.

The door widened a smidgen further, a glint of comprehension in the beady eyes. Doonaree, an ideal locale for a clandestine wedding— particularly a shotgun one.

'Aha,' he murmured, 'and when is the happy event?'

Our confusion was mistaken for reticence.

'Oh,' he exclaimed, 'pardon my decorum. I am Father O'Mahoney.'

The door was flung wide, and we were invited to enter the vestibule.

'Pray tell, when is the momentous day? And when do you wish for the ceremony to take place?'

'The day?' I queried.

'Yes,' he said, rubbing his protruding abdomen.

'No, Father,' my wife snapped, 'we are here regarding the positions.'

'Positions?'

'The notice,' she clarified, 'the teaching positions.'

'Ah. Are ye wed already?'

We both nodded in affirmation.

'Married,' he echoed, disappointment colouring his tone.

'More than two years, Father,' I offered.

A moment to re-evaluate.

'And you wish to teach in Doonaree?'

Our faces split into smiles as we nodded in agreement.

'Would you consider residing in the village?'

'Indeed, Father.'

'Very well. Return on Tuesday for an interview. Ask for Father Mullery.'

'Yes, Father. Thank you, Father.'

Teaching posts, as scarce as hens' teeth. To obtain two positions? In a single location? It exceeded our wildest dreams.

The interview was but a formality. The priest and the Master conferred privately in the parlour. A surreptitious observer might have witnessed their heads bent in proximity. At a casual glance, one might imagine a game of chess contested between two grandmasters. Upon closer inspection, the men were immersed in earnest conversation, fragments of which floated through the still air.

'Young couple.'

'Prepared to settle.'

'An asset to the staffroom.'
'No difficult questions necessary.'
'And Marcus, temper the Latin.'

We arrived punctually and were ushered into the parlour. The room was lavishly adorned: two ample bay windows draped in faded red curtains; a rich, red oriental rug; a glass chandelier dominating the ceiling, each lightbulb shimmering even though it was early afternoon. An ornate Tiffany lamp cast its light upon the marble-topped coffee table, encircled by four mahogany chairs upholstered in red. A baize-covered writing desk stood against one wall, while a grandfather clock provided a staccato tick-tock to punctuate the silences in conversation.

The meticulously arranged tea tray was a sight for weary eyes, and the travellers' gaze was drawn to the biscuits. Seated around the coffee table were a middle-aged, balding, overweight man dressed in a black suit and Roman collar, and an older, dignified gentleman with an abundant shock of white hair that belied his years.

Father Mullery, a compact, barrel-like man, approached us with hands outstretched. Introductions completed, he gestured towards the elder man. 'May I present Master Finnegan?'

The priest reached for the teapot, attending to the filling of cups, content to leave the remainder of the formalities to his esteemed school principal.

The elder man and the chair groaned in harmony as he gingerly rose to greet us.

'Marcus. Please call me Marcus. We're all colleagues here.'

'Ah, yes,' Father Mullery interjected. 'Marcus Tullius. Named after Cicero, you know?'

For a long time, we talked about matters far removed from teaching. Eventually, the Master deemed it necessary to at least attempt to fulfil the criteria of an interview.

In a voice imbued with gravitas, he inquired, 'What do you think of the blackboard vis-à-vis the overhead projector?'

The question was directed at me, and I responded diplomatically.

'Modern technology has its merits, but one cannot dismiss the success of traditional methodology. 'Talk and chalk' have endured since man first held a slate.'

The old man's eyes sparkled. *'Tabula rasa,'* he said. He proceeded to discuss the importance of physical education alongside academic disciplines. *'Mens sana,'* he declared, addressing no one in particular.

After consuming two cups of tea and several chocolate biscuits, we secured the positions. The 'interview' finally over, we shook hands with both the priest and the Master. Hail and farewell: *ave atque vale.*

'Can you believe that man?' I said to my wife as we drove away. 'Dying to flaunt his classical education. A relic. A dinosaur.' I mimicked his gravelly voice: 'The authority of those who teach is often an obstacle to those who want to learn.' We laughed together. Later, I wondered if he had been warning me about Jimmy Brady.

***

With his lanky frame, guileless face, shock of untamed black hair, and gap-toothed grin, Jimmy Brady embodied the ideal image of a healthy, large-boned, athletic country boy. Each school day, he strode down the mountain trailed by his two younger brothers and infant sister. They formed a single file and walked in silence. Sometimes, Jimmy cradled his baby sister in his powerful arms. They typically arrived before Master Finnegan had even opened the main gate. Teachers described Jimmy as the epitome of docility and the best-behaved boy in his class. What they refrained from mentioning was that Jimmy was a dunce – as dense as a block of wood. Of course, in the staff room, he was labelled 'pedagogically challenged,' 'intellectually deficient,' or 'on the spectrum.' But one thing was for sure – there was no teaching Jimmy Brady.

As a new teacher, I was receptive to advice but also imbued with youthful confidence. My training and natural communication skills would merge to make me the most exceptional teacher of all time. New techniques, innovative ideas, modern teaching methods – this traditional little school could benefit from a thorough shake-up. I had graduated top of my class in teacher training college, ready for any eventuality.

But nothing prepared me for Jimmy Brady.

Somehow, Jimmy had reached Fourth Class without learning a thing. He had successfully evaded any engagement with the written word. Mathematics appeared to him as a jumble of meaningless symbols. Dialogue and discourse were unattainable skills, except for the occasional, essential word.

I inherited Jimmy, along with thirty-six other pupils, from Mrs Burke. I swiftly built a rapport with 'my boys', except for young Jimmy who remained unmoved by his new teacher. He simply sat at his desk, observing the world around him without participating in it.

'How did Jimmy Brady fare in Third Class?' I asked Kitty Burke. Kitty's entrancing eyes peered at me from above her round, pink glasses, which teetered precariously on the tip of her nose. Her face appeared pinched, as though suffering a perpetual migraine. Brown hair, secured in a bun atop her head with hairpins and a pink butterfly clip, added extra height to her small frame. She habitually draped a grey Aran shawl over her shoulder. A snug green sweater, blue denim jeans tucked into black knee-high boots, completed her ensemble.

'Oh! I simply ignored him,' she responded haughtily. 'Leave him be, and he won't trouble you!' With a flourish of her shawl, she turned her back to me. 'You won't get lessons into our Jimmy,' she scoffed. 'You'd be fortunate to get a hello or a thank you.'

I devised a plan. Jimmy hailed from a farming background and was familiar with chickens and hens. Aiming not to embarrass him in front of his peers, I discreetly stowed photocopied pages from a Junior Infant textbook in my briefcase, awaiting the opportunity to introduce my recalcitrant pupil to the realm of reading.

Monday morning arrived, and I decided to forgo the standard English lesson, opting instead for a writing assignment. 'Compose a two-page essay on *An Adventure I had Last Weekend*,' I instructed the boys. Eagerly, thirty-six budding novelists began to write, while Jimmy sat upright at his desk, staring into space.

'Jimmy, would you please come here?' I requested.

Wordlessly, Jimmy approached my desk.

'How are you today, Jimmy?' I asked, trying to engage him. His response was a smile and a nod, but no words. Despite my attempts to ask about his weekend, he remained silent.

At this point, Robert Dooley raised his hand to ask for permission to use the restroom, followed by Tommy Kelly. I admonished them, reminding them they couldn't all go at once. Exasperated, I continued my conversation with Jimmy, asking him about helping at home and on the farm. His nods grew more definite as I homed in on poultry-related topics, such as geese, ducks, chicks, and hens.

During our one-sided conversation, Raymond Burke accused Willie Kennedy of cheating, resulting in a brief disruption. I sternly addressed the situation and urged the class to focus.

Returning my attention to Jimmy, I introduced the photocopied pages I had brought with me. 'I want you to look at the picture. Take your time. Look closely at it. Tell me what you see.'

Jimmy looked at the page. It contained a large-sized drawing of a hen in a farmyard setting. The photocopy was in colour. Plumage reddish-brown. Bright red comb. Yellow beak. Scattering of corn. Underneath. Large, bold letters. H-E-N.

Pointing to the picture, then to the letters, I said: 'Can you tell me what this is, Jimmy?'

His face showed puzzlement and then concern. I urged him to think about our conversation and the farmyard context, hoping for a breakthrough.

'Just one word, Jimmy,' I pleaded. 'We were talking about it, Jimmy. Think. Farmyard.'

Jimmy stared and stared. But no words passed his lips.

He hopped from foot to foot.

He was eager to please. He wanted to comply with my instructions. Words were beginning to form. Jimmy was about to answer. My heart soared. The breakthrough. One word.

An edifice could be built on a tiny platform.

'Tell me, Jimmy. What do you see in the picture?'

'A cock pheasant, Sir!'

***

Marcus was pleased to have a new male teacher on his staff. He found female teachers' conversations uninteresting and preferred the company of male colleagues. In fact, he had already started to consider grooming me as his successor.

One day, I approached him, seeking advice.

The knock on his door startled Marcus.

'I need to talk with you about Jimmy Brady,' I said, without any pleasantries.

'Indeed!' said Marcus.

'Just cannot get through to him. The boy does not seem to retain...'

'Silence is one of the great arts of conversation,' he interrupted. 'You will learn that God has a purpose for every child in this school. Even for Jimmy Brady. Not every child is gifted academically.'

He rummaged in his jacket pocket for his pipe. Without taking his eyes off me, he placed it on the table in front of him.

'A handful of people in this village have our level of education,' he continued, in a low voice. 'Ordinary country people. Farmers. The land gives them a living, not algebra, not history, not geography. They hold no store for transitive or intransitive verbs.'

'Even so,' I interjected. 'Fundamentals like reading and writing. Surely.'

'Young Henderson learned very quickly how to wield a butcher's pencil. Mossy Mullholland has no trouble with a bookie's pencil either. One of my past pupils, Tomsie Daly, is now the accountant in Hegerty's. Johnny Hegerty tells me that not a bag of grain, nor an ear of corn, nor a pinch of flour escapes Daly's notice and the books have never been as well serviced.'

'So, they learn, despite our best efforts,' I said.

The old schoolmaster took a plug of tobacco from his jacket pocket. A penknife magically appeared in his right hand. He began to scrape thin shards of moist tobacco into his fist. The mechanical act of kneading the shards into a ball helped him to gather his thoughts.

'They learn what is practical for them to learn. Sad truth is that most of them will never see the inside of a university. The inside of other institutions, more likely. Some of them won't even complete secondary school. They will snag turnips and plough fields and pick strawberries. Busy at harvest time. Draw dole and get drunk when things get quiet. Footsteps of their fathers. Three generations through my hands here. A handful made it to the big smoke.'

'But what will I say to Mrs Brady?' almost pleading now. 'I can't tell her that her boy is stupid. The parent teacher meeting will be coming up at mid-term.'

The ball of tobacco had made its way into the opening of his walnut pipe and was deftly packed with a gentle press of his thumb. A quick flick of a safety match set the leaves ablaze and soon the aroma of burning tobacco filled the air.

'Now tell me,' he said, blowing a plume of smoke over my head. 'Does Jimmy behave in class?'

'Of course,' I nodded, beginning to feel queasy. My eyes were stinging, and I searched the room for an open window.

'Does he sit at his desk? Does he bother anyone? Someone like Jimmy can distract. How do the others react?'

'Oh, no! Strange. The boys like him. They don't bother him, and he doesn't bother them.'

'Good. Good. Is he biddable? Do you ever ask him to...?'

He didn't get to finish the sentence. I was eager to escape into the fresh air. I stood up as if to leave.

'Jimmy is very reliable. I ask him to empty the bin in the evenings. He helps to clean the blackboard. He brings notes to the other teachers for me.'

'Mmmm,' said the old teacher. 'So, he is trustworthy. Solid. Dependable.'

I turned to leave. The frustration of not getting any assistance made me want to scream.

The last words I heard were: 'Nobody can give you wiser advice than yourself: *numquam labere, si te audies* – if you heed yourself, you'll never go wrong.'

At the upcoming parent-teacher meeting, I took Marcus's advice to heart. As I discussed Jimmy's performance with his mother, I highlighted his reliability and trustworthiness. Mrs Brady left the meeting beaming, and I felt a sense of accomplishment. I imagined her smiling at the other mothers. Delighted with her son. Really pleased. There would be apple pie with custard for an evening treat. Jimmy loves the custard. Such a good boy. Such a caring boy. And now the new young Master is so happy with him as well. Yes indeed! The height of praise! What was it he said? Must remember the exact words. Ah yes!

'Jimmy is a great boy to do a message.'

Although my initial attempts to teach Jimmy had been challenging, I learned that focusing on a student's strengths can sometimes yield better results than concentrating solely on academic achievement.

***

Years flowed by, and I found myself in the familiar parlour of the Parochial House once more. Though three Parish Priests had come and gone, the room had scarcely altered. The oriental red carpet was now supplanted by a luxurious pile adorned with garish purple blossoms, yet the glass chandelier clung askew and precariously to the ceiling, held by a mere three of its original four screws. Some bulbs were absent; the sparse remainder dimly glinted, vying with the late afternoon sun dancing upon the blue drapes that framed the bay windows.

I had entered this room on many occasions. The baize-covered writing desk, the coffee table, the mahogany chairs, and the ornate Tiffany lamp never failed to evoke memories of my inaugural visit. The grandfather clock had ceased to tick, and I longed for the steady pulse of its heartbeat. Alone I sat in the room, accompanied solely by my thoughts.

Time had hastened by. Retirement loomed ever closer. The principal's salary was more than sufficient, yet the prospect of solitude held little appeal. First, my dear wife. Then, Kitty. An improbable affair, extinguished as quickly as it had ignited, dismissed with a flourish of her shawl.

Father O'Shea, all bluster and bristle, burst into the room, clutching a sheaf of papers in one hand and a parcel in the other. 'Ah, there you are, Master, apologies for the delay. No time for tea, I fear. This sermon is particularly challenging, and His Lordship has requested that I stand in for O'Reilly in the neighbouring parish. Thus, full steam ahead we must go!'

'*Semper pergendum sine timore,*' I replied. 'One should always go forward without fear.'

I had never witnessed him operate at anything less than full steam. His abruptness was unsurprising, but I couldn't help wondering why he had summoned me this afternoon. Rising from my seat with some difficulty—arthritis, the doctor said, and wear and tear—I prepared to depart. My inquisitive expression reminded him of my visit's purpose.

'Ah, yes, Master. This arrived for you today.'

He pressed the parcel into my hands.

'As you can see, it is addressed to you, care of the Parochial House.'

Cloaked in unadorned, brown paper and heavily secured with sturdy, transparent tape, the parcel bore American stamps. The postmark indicated Washington D.C., a few days prior. Intrigued by the package's heft, my curiosity demanded immediate investigation. The priest, too, momentarily forgetting his packed schedule, eyed the parcel with suspicion.

'Should I open it here?' I inquired, adding, 'I haven't the faintest...'

'By all means, by all means,' urged the priest, removing the Tiffany lamp from the coffee table. I set the package down and tore through the wrapping.

It was a hardback book—wildlife photography. Together we stared at it, and after a few moments, I opened the cover.

Neat, blue handwriting penned a dedication.

*Grandpa said that you were
the best teacher he ever had.*

Very best wishes,

Mathew James Brady

Master Photographer.

The cover photograph showcased a breathtaking, wild bird in flight. Set against a hazy backdrop of fields and trees, the unmistakable plumage of a cock pheasant came sharply into focus.

A Splendid Day

The sun cast a shimmering, golden haze over the expansive Marble Hill beach, its languid warmth a sensual embrace that had been absent for far too long. It was a June Bank Holiday Monday, and Donegal seemed to have been spared the damp melancholy that plagued the rest of the country. He savoured a secret satisfaction, the knowledge that others were not as fortunate as he.

Together, he and his wife strolled across the sands, their footfalls five paces apart, leaving a trail of ephemeral memories in their wake. Benny, their black Labrador, frolicked at the water's edge, delighting in his newfound freedom, oblivious to the tension that hung between his two companions like a tattered shroud.

A symphony of sensations enveloped the couple: the scent of salt and seaweed mingling in the air, the coarse, gritty texture of sand beneath their feet, the taste of the briny sea breeze as it danced across their lips. Yet, amid the beauty of their surroundings, an impenetrable silence clung to them, a barrier that neither could breach.

He tried to pierce the quiet, his voice tentative, almost hesitant as he sought to fill the void that stretched between them.

'A writer, Colm Toibín, I think... once said that he loved the Irish summer,' he ventured. 'It was his favourite day of the year!'

A soft chuckle accompanied the words, but it was met with silence. Undeterred, he tried again.

'You can't beat Donegal on a fine summer's day!'

'Beautiful, isn't it?' she replied, her voice distant, a mere echo of the connection they once shared.

The air of melancholy that enveloped them was as palpable as the sea mist that hung on the breeze, the space between them an ocean of unspoken words and stifled emotions. As the sun dipped lower in the sky, casting long shadows across the sands, they found themselves perched on rocky thrones, the imposing monoliths an embodiment of the distance that had grown between them.

He sat upon his chosen stone, warmed by the sun's fading embrace, a sense of serenity washing over him like the gentle caress of the waves on the shore.

'Sit over here,' she said.

Perhaps she said: 'Why don't you sit over here?'; or 'Would you like to sit over here?'

'No,' he resisted.

'Sit over here'.

'I'm fine where I am,' he answered in an effort to placate her.

'There's no wind over here. I found a drier stone.'

Turning his head slightly, he saw that she was spreading a newspaper on the flat top of the rock beside her.

He thought about saying: 'If the stone is dry, why do you need the newspaper?' but he remained silent.

'Come over and sit here,' she said again.

His head a jumble of thoughts, he repeated, 'I'm fine where I am.'

'Come on, it's better over here.'

The tension simmered, the unresolved emotions churning like the tempestuous sea, neither willing to bridge the chasm that had formed between them.

He grappled with what he should do.

Slowly, he got up and went to the designated rock, the one draped with newspaper. He sat clumsily. The rock was too high. Uncomfortable. His legs did not dangle to the sandy surface. They hung like leaden weights, causing the muscles in his arse to bruise.

'My own rock is better,' he said, grumpily. He went back to where he had been.

Benny spotted a seagull and chased after it into the crashing waves. Tiny white clouds mushroomed on the mountains in the distance.

'It will rain before long,' he said. Rising from his seat, he whistled and shouted at the dog.

'Come here, you eejit! You're all wet!'

The dog skulked back dutifully, with his spine humped and his tail curled between his legs. The man grabbed his neck and roughly connected a lead to his collar. He cast a sidelong glance at his wife, her figure silhouetted against the fading light. The sun dipped lower still. A warm, golden glow suffused the sands, their beauty a stark contrast to the storm that raged within their hearts.

Wordlessly, he rose and made his way back to the car, with the dog in tow, straining on the leash. He opened the car door, heart heavy with the weight of unspoken truths and the knowledge that, even amid such splendour, the gulf that separated them seemed to have grown even wider.

A short while later, his wife folded the newspaper, tucked it under her arm and followed them.

The Café of Learning

The first light of dawn had barely begun to paint the sky with the softest hues of rose and gold when the doves in the University clock tower awoke. Their internal metronomes, delicate and precise as the inner workings of the clock itself, brought them to life in synchrony with the world around them. As they took flight, their white wings brushed against the air, casting a spell of tranquillity over the ancient stones of the university.

Below, the cobblestoned grounds lay in stillness, a hush that belied the cacophony of intellectual fervour that would erupt later in the day. The air was heavy with the scents of dew-kissed grass and the faintest trace of wood smoke from nearby chimneys. The atmosphere was pregnant with the promise of knowledge, a silent invocation to the gods of wisdom.

In the midst of this tableau, Claire, a young woman in her early twenties with dark, cascading curls, pedalled her bicycle towards the university café. The gentle sound of the wheels on the cobblestones punctuated the silence like a heartbeat, a living thrum that marked the rhythm of her days.

As Claire entered the café, she was greeted by the aroma of coffee beans and fresh pastries, a symphony of scents that mingled with the faint fragrance of old books and the distant, ever-present murmur of the sea. The café was her sanctuary, her very own ivory tower, in which she could live out her daydreams of romance and adventure.

She would dance among the tables and chairs, her movements as fluid and graceful as the notes of a sonata, her laughter like the tinkling of bells. With each sweep of her arm, she conjured a world of elegance and beauty, a world in which she was the belle of the ball, dancing with the heroes of literature and film.

As she moved, the air around her was filled with the aroma of roses and candle wax, the soft strains of violins and the rustle of silk. The touch of her fingers on the broom handle was as tender as the touch of a lover, and the taste of anticipation lingered on her lips, as sweet as the nectar of the gods.

With each pirouette, Claire transcended the ordinary, transforming her humble café into a palace of the imagination. She was a swan gliding upon a glassy lake, a star shining in the firmament of dreams. Her world was a tapestry of colour and light, woven from the threads of longing and desire.

Claire would never know the joy of reading words on a page. But a philomath will not be thwarted in her quest for learning.

And as the first students and teachers began to trickle in, their voices a babble of ideas and arguments, Claire's lessons began. She listened with rapt attention, her mind drinking in their words like a parched desert receiving the first rain. She feasted upon the taste of knowledge, savouring each morsel as it nourished her soul and expanded her horizons.

For Claire, the café was more than just a place to serve coffee and pastries; it was the gateway to a world of possibility, a world where she could spread her wings and soar like the doves in the university clock tower, her heart as light and free as the wind that carried them aloft.

The Picnic

'For the record, Mr Conway waives the right to have a solicitor present.'

The formalities over, she let her tongue trace the freshly applied lipstick, smiled, and in the friendliest voice she could muster, said:

'Now let's go over your version of events again.'

The bald head stirred from under his black fleece. First one eye, then the other appeared and blinked open. As his face emerged, Nancy could see that he wore a red tee-shirt.

'But I've already been through it with the other officers.'

Under the unrelenting gaze of the cold, fluorescent light, the air in the room seemed to condense, heavy with the weight of his words. The scent of stale coffee and the lingering, acrid odour of sweat clung to the atmosphere, a testament to the hours spent in the small, confining space.

She could see that he was exhausted. She thrust a bottle of chilled water towards him.

'Here. Drink this. I want to hear your story at first hand. The details. I'm here to help you, Mr Conway. William. Can I call you Bill?'

'Liam.'

'Okay, Liam.'

She paused. Took a deep breath.

'Now, you were on the beach. Take it from there.'

Reluctantly, like a child asked to recite a badly learned poem in school, the old man began his story.

'Yeah, we were on the beach...'

'We?'

'Margaret and me.'

'Margaret?'

'Yes. And Jessie was making sandcastles. Running in and out to the water.'

'Jessie?'

'My granddaughter. She loves the beach. Never stands still.'

Arching an eyebrow, Nancy struggled to mask the look of disbelief on her face.

'What did ye have for your picnic?'

'Brown bread, cream cheese. And a flask of coffee.'

'Mmm. Wasn't it cold on the beach? Middle of January?'

'Yeah. We wrap up well, Margaret and me. We love picnics. Margaret says: "No such thing as bad weather, only bad clothes!"'

His body shook with the memory.

'No plastic knifes or forks for Margaret. She spreads a tablecloth. Does it in style, d'you understand?'

His eyes wandered to the ceiling. He peered as if looking at a cinema screen on which these events were unfolding.

'We spread out all the food. And takeaway cups. We always drink coffee from takeaway cups. You get more coffee.'

Staring upwards like a martyred saint. The whites of his eyes gave him a ghostly aspect. Nancy tried to make eye contact.

'Let's get back to today. You were drinking coffee and...'

'I saw the Alsatian, first. Black Alsatian. Fierce looking. Immediately worried for Jessie.'

His eyes blazing now. A look of alarm. He stared not at her, but through her.

'"Jessie," I called. "Come over here this instant." Of course, the child paid no heed. She had her bucket. Filling the moat. A castle, d'you understand? A sandcastle.'

'The dog approached,' Liam continued, his voice subdued and hesitant. 'I called for Margaret, told her to keep an eye on Jessie. The sand was cold beneath my feet as I moved, grains of it scratching my skin, but my mind was focused on the dog.'

Nancy's gaze bore into him, her eyes the colour of a deep winter sky. She could almost hear the waves crashing on the shore, feel the biting wind that whipped around them. 'And then what happened?' she asked, her voice almost a whisper, as if afraid to shatter the fragile world he was weaving.

'The dog's growl, it was... it was guttural. Almost like it reverberated through the air, you know? The fur on its back bristled, standing on end. I tried to step in between it and Jessie, but it lunged before I could do anything.'

Nancy's fingers tightened on the edge of the table, knuckles turning white. 'Did it... Did it hurt Jessie?' she asked.

A shudder coursed through Liam's body, the memory of the moment overwhelming him. 'No, no, thank God. It turned on me instead. I could feel its teeth sinking into my arm, the pain... indescribable. But I couldn't think about that. I had to protect Jessie.'

She studied him for a moment, the stress etched into his features, the agony of his memory laid bare before her. Then, quietly, she said, 'What about the owner? The owner of the dog?'

He looked up at her, his eyes brimming with fear.

'The man appeared out of nowhere. Walking across the strand. Making a beeline directly for us. Strutting. As if he owned the place. Waving his arms. Shouting.'

'What was he shouting about?'

'I don't know. He was foreign. He grabbed the dog and flung a ball out to sea. The dog raced away.'

'What did this person do then?'

'He stood over us. His shadow blocked the sunlight. It's a big enough beach. Why did he have to stand there?'

A look of terror passed over his face.

'He was shouting at me.'

'Can you remember anything he said?'

'No. I told you. It was foreign. He was just shouting.'

'And... em... What, do you think, was he saying?'

'He was looking for money. Demanding. He... he wanted my wallet, d'you understand? He was going to rob us.'

'Oh. I see. And... ah... at this stage, where was the Alsatian?'

'In the sea. Seagulls. The Alsatian is gunning for them.'

Breathing heavily now. Reliving everything. Words come out in separate gasps.

'Watching out for Jessie. Hoping the Alsatian will stay distracted. The further out it swims, the safer...'

His voice tailed off. The glazed look.

Nancy knew she could not afford to let him exhaust himself. Yet, she wanted detail. She had to move his story on. It was a delicate balance.

'So, Liam. The dog is in the sea. This foreign fella is shouting at you. Then what happened?'

'He kept asking for money. My wallet. At one point, he turned to look out towards the sea. I stabbed him.'

'You stabbed him?'

'Yes. I had the knife, d'you understand? The breadknife.'

'You *stabbed* him with the breadknife?'

'Yes. Yes, I did.'

'And what happened then?'

'I heard a hiss from his side. Air from his lung, d'you understand? Punctured, like a tyre.'

The old man made a hissing sound.

'And there was blood; lots of blood.'

He rubbed his fists against the insides of his thighs. Then, he made to stand up. The uniformed guard moved quickly towards him to apply some pressure to his shoulders. Nancy gave him a sharp reprimand with her eyes. Shrugging, the uniform went back to his position at the door. The old man sagged into his chair again.

'And he roared. He screamed. He was screeching and clutching his side. Staggered backwards, a look of horror in his eyes. Shock. He was walking... no... running backwards. Then, he slumped to the ground. The Alsatian heard the cries. Time stood still. The man squirmed, screamed, on the sand. All senses alert, the dog bounded in slow motion towards him.'

'The man was trying to rise to his knees. I was getting up to help him. The Alsatian finally arrived, d'you understand? He whined. Licked the man's face. Curled up against him. Placed his body between me and his master. Stared at me. Defiantly. Slobbering spit. Growling. Fierce fangs. I couldn't move. I reached for Margaret's hand. She was in shock. Rooted to the spot. "Dear God. I can't see Jessie!" she cried. "Sweet Jesus, Jessie. Where are you?"'

Liam put his head in his hands. Visibly tiring. Energy draining from his pallid face. Shaking head from side to side.

'I need some rest,' he said, his voice pleading. 'I need to put my head down and sleep.'

'Just another few minutes, Liam. I have to get the facts. I need the facts.'

Liam raised his eyes. A mixture of confusion and weariness. She could not see any remorse. He was blasé – matter of fact. No trace of guilt. No regret. *Is this a cold-blooded killer?*

'I looked into the Alsatian's eyes and I said: "I hope you haven't hurt my Jessie." I couldn't go near the man to help him. I took out my mobile and rang. It was an hour before the ambulance arrived.'

He unfolded his palms, like a priest in the confessional. 'And that's what happened, d'you understand?' he croaked, his voice thick with emotion.

There was a knock on the door. A uniformed guard whispered something into Nancy's ear.

'We'll take a quick break, Liam,' she said, and she rose from her chair.

As Nancy left the interview room, the scent of the sea lingered in her nostrils, the taste of salt on her lips. She had listened to Liam's story, entered his world for a moment, and understood him better for it. Perhaps, just perhaps, there was a place for her here, a way to use her empathy to bridge the gap between herself and those she sought to understand. The thought of the transfer application, still sitting on her desk, seemed suddenly less urgent.

The uniformed guard pointed to a phone receiver on his desk. Nancy picked it up. 'Mr Geraghty,' she said. 'Are you absolutely sure about this?'

A few minutes later, Nancy was back in the interview room. She regarded the man with a mixture of compassion and disbelief. 'Liam,' she began, her voice as soft as the distant echo of the ocean waves, 'I'm sorry, but the truth is that when the ambulance arrived, there was no Alsatian. No Jessie. No Margaret. Just you, and the body.'

He stared at her, his eyes haunted by phantoms.

'Margaret and Jessie are no longer with us,' Nancy continued. 'The car crash took them from you, and I understand how much that hurts.'

In the echoes of his shattered heart, the gulls cried, their mournful calls a keening lament for the life he had known.

'But the picnic, the Alsatian, the man,' he insisted, his voice a thin thread fraying at the edges. 'It all happened, d'you understand?'

Nancy leaned forward, her gaze never wavering from his. 'Liam, I believe that you believe it was real. But we must face the truth, as hard as it may be. We're here to help you, but you have to let us. You've got to accept what's happened and allow us guide you through it.'

'No. No. Jessie was there. Playing. And Margaret. We were having a picnic, d'you understand? And everything was... everything would have been all right if he hadn't attacked. Why didn't he just leave us alone?'

His head slumped into his arms.

'Can I sleep now? I'm very tired.'

'Yes, okay, Liam.' She resisted the urge to pat him on the shoulder. 'We'll get a cup of tea for you. You can rest. Even though you said you didn't want one, I've called a solicitor to talk with you. He will be here shortly. Then, I'm sorry, but we'll have to go through it from the start again. I need to check some facts.'

'But I've told you all I know.'

'Liam, when I left the room, I spoke with your neighbour on the phone. Mr Geraghty in Number 2.'

'Henry?'

'Yes. Mr Henry Geraghty. Do you know Mr Geraghty?'

'Yes. Henry and I have been friends for years.'

'The thing is, Mr Geraghty tells me that your wife, Margaret, and your granddaughter were killed in a car crash last summer. A head on collision. The driver of the other car, a rental, survived. He was a foreign gentleman.'

'Oh, no. No. We were having a picnic, d'you understand? It was a fine day. Jessie loves the sea. And Margaret does picnics in style.'

A Lesson in Regret

Tony McCarthy's tongue felt like sandpaper scraping against the roof of his mouth. The throbbing in his temples was worse than usual, and he swore for the umpteenth time that he would quit drinking. But not today. First, he had to get his body to cooperate with him. He adjusted his eyes to the glaring sunlight filtering through the blinds into his room.

I don't have blinds in my bedroom, he realised with a jolt.

He was sprawled on the sofa in his office. He had slept in his rumpled suit. Delicately placing one foot on the wooden floor, he eased himself first into a sitting position where he paused. Then he stood up. His other foot hit an empty wine bottle, one of many that littered the surface. Overturned beer cans drooled on the expensive rug. A sickly odour rose from the oozing dregs, coagulating ash, and vomit. An upturned ashtray had deposited its contents into the sticky slime.

'Good heavens!' he muttered.

He rubbed his hands through his dishevelled hair and pressed the palms hard against his temples. It didn't stop the throbbing, but it gave him a certain amount of balance, enough he hoped, to make it to the bathroom. When he saw the sink, the dry retches began. No matter how hard he tried, he couldn't stop the convulsions which overcame him. He had no food to throw up, which led him to speculate about when he had last eaten.

Did I eat yesterday, or did I already deposit the contents of my stomach elsewhere?

Involuntary seizures and spasms gripped him. He heaved and heaved until his lungs hurt. Finally, the dry retching stopped. He grappled with his jacket and threw it out the bathroom door. Then he took the rest of his clothes off and forced himself to stand under the shower.

He cursed, as the streams of cold water burnt his skin.

The students in Lecture Hall 222 were used to their tutor being late. Some had already left, and the remaining few barely raised an eyebrow when the dishevelled Irishman swept into the lecture hall. He was more unkempt than usual. He placed his briefcase on the table next to the lectern and then faced his audience. The students waited for his first words. They could usually judge the state of his mind and guess at his nocturnal activities by his first utterance. Was he going to be coherent and logical today? Was he going to rant?

Tony felt that he had, to use an Irish phrase, 'scrubbed up well!' His hangover was worse than usual, but the two stiff brandies that he managed to hold down were working their magic.

He began to speak. A brilliant orator. No notes. No documents. *My audience will be enraptured.*

The students had become used to the eccentricities of their Irish tutor. He never failed to surprise them in some way. They rarely knew in what direction he was going to lead them. He was different from all the other teachers. He appeared to make up his lectures as he went along. Yet, he opened their minds by challenging them to think. 'Expect the unexpected,' was his introduction to them during their first lecture. 'Always, expect the unexpected.'

One or two had already complained to Professor Bichon about the erratic behaviour of their English tutor. Some fellow lecturers expressed surprise that Tony McCarthy was still allowed to deliver lectures in an unseemly, inebriated state.

'Once upon a time,' he began. 'Once upon a time.'

He paused. He watched as the students sat expectantly.

'Once upon a time,' he said again. 'Four little words. What do they signify? Yes, of course, we've heard these four words many times. Those of you who were lucky enough to have a parent to read to you when you were little will remember these words from your childhood. Once Upon a Time... the beginning of a fairy tale. Once Upon a Time. The words that open untold vistas of myths and legends, the world of imaginary characters: witches and goblins, fairies and leprechauns, giants and trolls, princes and princesses.'

'Once Upon a Time. It is the 'Open Sesame' to the world of fairy tales.'

'But,' and here Tony, squeezed his eyes shut and held his hand aloft, commanding attention. He failed to notice the last of the students leave the hall.

'What if I were to tell you that the greatest Irish writer who ever lived chose these four words to begin the landmark book of twentieth-century literature?'

Eyes closed, Tony imagined he had their full attention now. He pictured the students shifting uneasily in their seats and asking: 'Where is he going with this? 'Once Upon a Time...?'; 'Open Sesame...?'; 'Greatest book of twentieth-century literature...?'

He was blind to the fact that he was delivering his lecture to an empty hall.

'Listen, now, and I'll tell you the opening lines,' he said, and without a book in his hand, he recited:

'Once upon a time and a very good time it was there was a moocow coming down along the road and this moocow that was coming down along the road met a nicens little boy named baby tuckoo... His father told him that story: his father looked at him through a glass: he had a hairy face. He was baby tuckoo. The moocow came down the road where Betty Byrne lived: she sold lemon platt.'

Tony stopped his recitation at this point.

'Thus starts one of the greatest books of the twentieth century. And his name?'

Doing his best Bond impression, he said: 'My name is Joyce. James Joyce.'

'You have just been listening to the opening lines of *The Portrait of the Artist as a Young Man.*'

'Anthony?'

Startled.

He opened his eyes. The dignified figure of Professor Bichon approached.

'Ah, Professor, come to hear the Joyce lecture?' said Tony.

'No,' said the Professor, 'I've come to have a talk with you. Gather up your things, and we'll walk to my office.'

Bloods

When Dr McCawley settled into the chair beside me, an air of solemnity enveloped the room, and I knew that the news he was about to impart would be far from comforting. I could perceive the faint aroma of disinfectant that pervaded the small, meticulously ordered examination room, and the relentless ticking of the wall clock seemed to reverberate in my ears.

'Mr. Smyth,' he began, his voice measured and imbued with gravitas, 'the good news is that if we address this issue in a timely manner, the liver and kidney functions might not be adversely affected.'

'Liver and kidney?' I echoed, my heart skipping a beat.

Dr McCawley sighed. 'It's difficult to elucidate,' he continued, his voice maintaining a professional tone. 'Your blood results indicate a significant spike.'

'Spike?' I asked, my voice barely a whisper.

Turning the monitor towards me, he pointed to a graph. 'Two months ago, your readings were within the normal range. Now, an abnormal level of cortisol. It appears the bone marrow is accelerating its activity, resulting in elevated leukocytes.'

'Leukocytes?' I queried, my mind reeling from the revelation.

'Yes, white blood cells,' he affirmed, his eyes focused on the data before him. He regarded me over the rim of his glasses, his expression one of genuine concern. 'You haven't resumed drinking, have you?'

'No, Doctor,' I replied, my voice barely audible.

'And your cholesterol has increased significantly. This doesn't bode well, Mr. Smyth.'

'My cholesterol was always within normal limits,' I murmured, meekly.

'Yes, I'm aware,' he conceded. 'Therefore, I recommend that we arrange for a series of tests, post-haste.' Speaking into his Dictaphone, he said, 'Tests for Mr. Robert Smith – S-M-I-T-H.'

'No, no,' I interjected. 'Smyth with a y.'

A look of horror passed over the doctor's face, and he swallowed hard. Recovering his composure, he whispered, 'My goodness, Smyth with a y? Incorrect blood samples.'

'The wrong blood samples?' I inquired, a glimmer of hope emerging.

'The incorrect test results,' he confirmed.

'I'm okay?' I asked, scarcely daring to believe it.

'You are perfectly fine,' Dr McCawley reassured me, his voice tinged with relief and a hint of embarrassment. 'I apologise for summoning you here.'

As he led me to the door, he remarked, 'Now, I must repeat this process with the other gentleman.'

'Good luck with that,' I replied, the ghost of a smile playing on my lips as I exited the office, my heart lighter than it had been in what felt like an eternity.

The Three Amigos

You never could predict with Billy. He'd share a tale with a straight face, and you'd be convinced it was the truth. Only when laughter erupted afterward would you realise your gullibility. Everyone in the pub seemed to have his measure. But not me. His stories were woven with enough truth to reel me in. Before I knew it, I was so engrossed with the narrative that the part of my brain crying 'nonsense!' simply shut down.

Now, he was telling me about Malachy McCluskey. I knew Malachy, and while I didn't know specifics, I had heard about his health issues. Billy had sidled up to the bar.

'A fine one about McCluskey,' he said, luring me in.

I must admit I'd had a skinful. I was drinking more as Christmas approached; we all were.

'Malachy?' I asked. 'What about him?'

Billy sat on the empty stool beside me.

'I don't mind if I do,' he said, nodding at my nearly empty glass.

So what if it cost me a pint to hear his story?

He remained silent until two frothy pints settled on the counter.

'He was due for a hospital visit to have a cardio-conversion done.'

'A cardio-conversion?' I inquired.

'Yeah, a cardio-conversion,' said Billy. 'That's where they give the old ticker a shock to restore its rhythm to tickity-boo again.'

He gestured with his hands as if he were a giant panda embracing a tree, mimicking the application of defibrillator paddles, like you see on television dramas.

'I wasn't aware his ticker was out of sync,' I admitted.

'Oh, you wouldn't notice it much on flat ground. But you should have seen him on stairs.'

He filled his lungs and puffed out his cheeks.

'So, what happened to Malachy?' I pressed.

'The strangest thing,' said Billy.

I cradled my pint and rested my chin on the glass rim, intent on concentrating on every word.

'His brother owns a farm in Headford,' said Billy, 'and Malachy went for a visit. I suppose to inform his brother about the upcoming hospital procedure. *Away up with ya,* said the brother, and the two trekked up the fields to where sheep were penned – a narrow strip of land, grass nibbled to its roots, and brown earth peering through. Three strands of barbed wire encircled the field. A gentle ticking sound could be heard from the little red battery placed at the foot of a pillar that supported the iron bar gate. *Place your hand on that fence,* instructed the brother. Unthinking, Malachy touched the wire. Would you believe the electric shock set his hair standing on end? He gave a quare hop, too!'

Billy sprang upright as he spoke, his eyes bulging and lips contorting into a grotesque sneer.

'Was he alright?' I inquired.

'Alright?' Billy retorted. 'Never better. They didn't need to bring him to the hospital at all. Now, he can run up the stairs without a bother.'

I waited for Billy to buy his round. Alas, I was out of luck.

A few weeks later, Billy was dead. Fell down the stairs. Everyone at the funeral claimed he was sober at the time.

I didn't tell anyone, but Billy called me one night shortly before he died. He had another tall tale for me, which I didn't believe. It seems he found a leaflet. 'Why Me? – A Questionnaire.' You know the type. *Is drinking making your home life unhappy? Do you drink because you are shy around others? Do you drink alone? If you answer 'YES' to three or more of these questions, you are undoubtedly an alcoholic.*

I told him that half the country would be alcoholics if they answered those questions honestly.

I was perched on the edge of my bed. It was late at night. I shivered.

His call left me uneasy. The last thing he said to me was that he planned to check himself in. I laughed. My bullshit detector was finely attuned for this one. I told him I'd meet him for a few nice pints the following evening.

Billy didn't show.

The next time I saw him, he lay in a coffin. Looking as well as ever. Just, he was dead.

'You are the last of the Three Amigos,' his wife said to me.

I hadn't considered it until then.

When I first moved into the neighbourhood, there were Bob and Billy and me. We used to visit each other's homes. Like young lads. 'Can Billy come out to play?' Once we were together, our wives didn't mind. We were company for each other.

Bob had gone in for a simple operation. Gallstones, I believe. Everything went well. He was due out after the weekend. Bank Holiday Monday. He contracted an infection and died.

Billy came to my house to tell me. We drank brandy. We pooled our money to purchase booze for the wake and funeral.

'Can't have people visiting his home without something to wet their whistles,' Billy declared.

The Two Amigos didn't have the same ring to it. After a while, we forgot about the nickname.

Now, I attempt to recall these things. The anaesthetist asks my name and date of birth.

'I told you before,' I snap.

I'm growing irritated with his questions. I want to tell him I am the last of the Three Amigos. He's uninterested. He just wants me to keep repeating my name and birthdate. I want to tell him about Bob and Billy. And how Billy got the procedure name wrong. We could have laughed about that. When my surgeon informed me I needed a cardioversion, I told him it was a cardio-*conversion*.

The anaesthetist asks my name and birthdate again.

'Amigo,' I whisper as I slip into a deep sleep.

The Alpine Air

It was an impromptu decision for them to visit the second highest mountain in Austria. Rusty didn't know what to expect. Sheila had announced first thing in the morning that she wanted to explore some of the tours in the brochure.

'Almost a week of our holidays gone,' she said. 'Nothing but eating, drinking, and sleeping. We could have done that at home.'

'That's what you're supposed to do on holidays,' Rusty grumbled, the whiskey from the night before playing havoc with the inside of his head.

Sheila sighed, her exasperation evident.

'We work hard enough the rest of the year,' continued Rusty. 'What's wrong with letting our hair down for a bit during the holidays?' He said this without conviction. Last thing Rusty wanted this morning was an argument. And this squabble had been well aired.

'Surely you can think of better things to do?' came the return volley. 'What's the point in coming to Austria and going to Irish pubs all the time? Did you ever consider finding out what the locals eat or drink?'

'There's nothing wrong with steak and potatoes,' Rusty replied defensively, 'only you have to keep reminding them to cook the meat on the inside.'

'Well, I'm going to the Wildspitze this morning, whether you're coming or not,' Sheila declared, her tone final.

A quick shower, a rub of the razor across his chin, a rushed cup of black coffee later, and they were on the tour bus to Vent. Sheila had purchased the tickets in the hotel lobby.

'There are three stages to the ascent,' she informed him. 'I bought tickets for all three. Might as well see the whole mountain as we've come this far.'

Sheila read the brochure notes again, careful to shield them from Rusty.

'The Wildspitzlift is a two-man chairlift leading from the hamlet of Vent up to 2,350 metres above sea level. The top station of the lift is the starting point for many walks and hikes, including up onto the Wildspitze mountain. The journey up on the lift is an experience in itself.'

As the bus moved towards Vent, Rusty's stomach tightened in dread, the beginnings of a panic attack bubbling beneath the surface. He didn't want to disappoint Sheila, but his fear of heights and the whiskey-induced fog clouding his mind made the prospect of the mountain ascent even more daunting.

When they arrived at the cable car station in Vent, Rusty excused himself to find a toilet. He didn't want to be caught short midway on the journey up the mountain. Bad enough to deal with his vertigo, without having to worry about his bladder as well. A few years ago, he couldn't even face the prospect of getting on an airplane. He never spoke about the incident, but when he was younger, something happened involving a small plane that scarred him for life. For over twenty years, he had refused to fly.

Now that he was nearing retirement, he began to take the first tentative steps to make up for lost time. His doctor prescribed tablets to calm his nerves during a flight. He quickly discovered that a few miniature bottles of whiskey, coupled with the tablets, helped him to forget his anxiety. If he had this cocktail, he could fly anywhere.

His fear of heights was rarely put to the test. Rusty learned that once he prepared properly, he could do most of the things he dreaded. When he had time to plan, he was careful not to drink too much the night before, he kept his medication close at hand, he controlled his breathing, and he steeled himself mentally for the ordeal ahead.

This expedition had come out of the blue. Sheila was independent enough to follow through on her threat to go alone. The prospect of mooching around the hotel all day didn't appeal to him. Neither did the lecture he would receive when she came back. He decided that the mountain trip would be the lesser of two evils.

He had just stepped into the cable car when he realised three things: In his rush to get ready, he had forgotten to take his morning set of pills. He began to feel tense and breathless. Secondly, he forgot to bring along his 'secret' stash of Valium; his fall-back vial of relievers that helped him to take the edge off in stressful situations. The vial was resting in the right-hand pocket of his leather jacket, which he had hung in the hotel wardrobe the night before. Thirdly, he remembered his hangover and his heart pounded a little quicker. All the weapons in his armoury had been discarded or ignored. He was defenceless. The certainty overcame him that he was going to have a panic attack.

Too late. The cable car had begun its ascent. In Rusty's mind, the sardine can was dangling by a piece of thread over the trees. He gripped the leather loop hanging from the roof, his knuckles white, as the car lurched and swayed its way from stanchion to stanchion, heading up higher and higher into the mountain. There were no more than seven people on board, mainly noisy teenagers with skis.

The air inside the cable car felt thick, heavy with the weight of his anxiety. The scent of pine trees and damp earth wafted in, mingling with the faint smell of sweat from the other passengers. The sounds of excited chatter and laughter bounced off the walls, reverberating in Rusty's head, only adding to his distress.

Sheila, on the other hand, marvelled at the breath-taking view, oblivious to her husband's growing panic.

'Oh, look,' she said, pointing at the scenery far below. 'Are those sheep or goats?'

Rusty, unable to bear the sight of the ground so far away, muttered a curse under his breath. His heart pounded in his chest, and he could taste the acrid bile that rose in his throat as he fought to keep his nausea at bay.

The journey didn't last long. They arrived at the first stopping station. Rusty's sense of relief was palpable. He had survived, without having a full-blown panic incident. The uniformed attendant helped people to disembark, and he directed them to an enclosed, railed walkway. Then, two at a time, he brought the passengers around a corner. To Rusty's horror, the attendants were assisting the passengers onto the next leg of the journey. Before he knew it, Rusty was sitting on a wooden bench, a metal bar had clamped down in front of him. He was swinging with his legs dangling in the open air. The cable car, with its outer shell, had afforded some protection or, at least, the illusion of some protection. Now, there was nothing between Rusty and the sweet earth below, except the narrow wooden plank on which he and Sheila sat.

'Oh, my good gawd,' he declared, 'I can't stand this.'

Sheila looked on in disbelief as she saw her panic-stricken husband squirm and swivel uncomfortably.

'If you keep twisting and turning, you'll knock the two of us into kingdom come,' she said, calmly.

'Jaysus, Mary and Joseph!' he cried. 'Let me get off.'

'Don't be silly, Rusty. You can't get off. It'll only take a minute or two and then we'll be there.'

'Oh, Jaysus. Why did you bring me up here?'

'Can't you just take a few deep breaths? Breathe in and out, slowly. In through your nose, out through your mouth. Take in the view. Look! What are those things down there?'

Sheila was fascinated to know whether the white dots below were patches of snow or mountain animals.

'It's amazing, isn't it?' she cried. 'Up amongst the clouds. See the snow! It's like as if we flew from summer into winter. I'm glad now that I brought my coat.'

'I can't look,' cried Rusty, his face plunged into his hands. 'Oh... gawd. When will it end?'

'We're coming to the next station, now I think,' said Sheila. 'You see? We're climbing up steeply.'

The ski-lift was approaching the brow of the hill. Suddenly, the chair crested the sharp ridge and then plunged to the other side. As far as the eye could see, there was nothing but more cable wire, more pylons and no sign of a stopping point.

Rusty's stomach lurched to his chest.

'Oh, Christ!' he groaned. 'There's no end to it. There's no sign of any station.'

It was true. The electric cable stretched from pylon to pylon, until it disappeared behind a cover of cloud.

The cable car was going downhill now having crested the ridge. This increased the sense of exposure. Popping over the top had given him a face-full of Alpine air and Rusty began to feel dizzy. He reached out his hand to hold onto Sheila.

'Get away from me,' she shrieked, and she pulled herself to the furthest end of the plank. 'Don't touch me!' she shouted. 'Keep your hands to yourself.'

Rusty recoiled.

'Oh, Jaysus,' he said. 'What if we slip off?'

'Don't,' she said.

Rusty pulled off his jacket. He threw it over his head. Then he started to count. Backwards.

'1,000, 999, 998 ...'

His knuckles were white as he gripped the edge of the wooden plank with one hand and the metal, restraining bar with the other.

Sheila huddled in a ball as far away from him as possible. The look on her face was a mixture of fear, disgust, and loathing. *You coward. You weakling. You drunk. Well, you're not going to drag me down with you.*

Finally, the lift reached the station. Rusty jumped off and ran for the toilet. The smell of vomit and stale alcohol made him retch again.

'Oh, Jaysus,' he said. 'How am I going to get back down?'

His mind turned to tranquilisers and alcohol, neither of which was available. The bar was closed. The little coffee shop didn't even have a wine licence.

'Where can I get a brandy?' his thoughts pestered.

'There's a beautiful panoramic restaurant open at the next stage,' said Sheila, when he came back. 'Stage three, at the top of the mountain. Listen.' And she began to read from the brochure.

'Next to the top of the Wildspitzlift is the panoramic café, Stablein, a self-service restaurant with a large sunny terrace.'

Rusty was incredulous. 'If you think that I'm getting back onto that plank, you've another think coming!'.

Already, the skiers were queuing to get on to the ski-lifts.

'There's no way in hell that I'm going up any further,' he said. 'I need to get a drink. Then I'm hiring a jeep or a truck to take me down from here.'

The lady in the ticket booth shook her head.

'The only way down is the way you came up.'

Rusty went back to the toilet.

He reappeared ten minutes later, resigned to his fate. He had no choice but to face the ordeal of the return journey again.

'If we have to do this, let's do it fast,' he said, and headed to the exit. Sheila, her plans thwarted, bristled with indignation as she followed.

He forced himself over to the embarking station, where the wooden benches slowly arrived to circle before heading back out again. The attendant held his hand to steady him. Rusty's face was a study in terror. He gripped the metal restraining bar and positioned himself on the edge of the wooden bench. Without a word, Sheila accepted the outstretched hand of the attendant and settled herself on the bench, as far apart from her husband as possible.

Rusty's panic attack intensified. The thin, cold Alpine air left a bitter taste on his tongue, and the smell of snow seemed to amplify his anxiety.

'Oh Gawd. Get me out of this and I swear I'll never drink again. Gawd, get me down from here and I'll go to Mass every Sunday. Lord, anything. Just get me down from here.'

Sheila never spoke.

Snivelling little man. What did I ever see in you? How did I put up with you for all those years?

By the time it came to the transfer into the cable car, Rusty had expended all his energy. He clung to the walls of the cable car and when it finally arrived back at the ground station, he almost hugged the earth with relief.

'Never again,' he said. 'Never again.'

Before they got back on the tour bus, Rusty had to have a few drinks.

'A brandy or two, for medicinal purposes,' he explained.

They sat on the veranda of the little roadside bar, which snuggled under the imposing mountain that towered towards the sky. Rusty had completely recovered his composure. He made comments about the different tourists who were queuing to get on the cable car. Now and again, he offered comforting words of advice to those who appeared nervous about the adventure.

Sheila sipped at her glass of white wine. Wearing sunglasses, with her yellow, wide-brimmed sunhat shading her face, she felt like a movie star. She stared absently up at the Wildspitze. Her mind was busy making arrangements.

The pictures in the living room can stay. He can keep the oversized TV and music system. The small TV in the kitchen will do me nicely. My brother's white van can take my settee – yes, MY settee – to Mum's house. Great opportunity to declutter. I've been meaning to do it for ages.

Wonderful how the Alpine air helps to clarify your thinking.

An Inconvenient Time

The melancholy of the dimly lit bar enveloped me as I approached, the air thick with the fug of cigarette smoke and the stench of despair. The amber glow of the whiskey bottles lining the shelves behind the counter cast a spectral sheen on the patrons, each one nursing their drink as if it were a balm for a lifetime of misery. The murmur of hushed conversations and the sombre drone of the jukebox playing an old blues song created an ambience that was almost suffocating. It was the kind of place where the soul was laid bare, where everyone sought refuge in the shadows.

The stranger was perched on my high stool, a dark overcoat, crumpled and slept-in, stretched across his broad shoulders. In the mirror, I could see his black tie askew, the top three buttons of his stained, white shirt undone. A while since he had seen the inside of a barber's, his greasy, grey hair curled up at his neck, a week's growth of stubble on his chin. An unpleasant odour mingled with the smell of stale beer made me recoil.

His elbows anchored to the counter, he clutched at his beer glass as though it could warm him. Hunched over, despondent, the hangdog look on his pained face was that of a condemned man. I'd seen that look before—every morning when I shaved.

I ordered whiskey—neat—and thought about walking away, but there was something about this stranger that held me captive. I moved closer to him, the air of intrigue and mystery growing thicker as I did so.

A low growl escaped his lips, his voice gravelly and raw. 'A split second. Changes everything!' he said.

I wasn't in the mood for hard luck yarns, but I couldn't resist the allure of this stranger's story.

Call it the thrill of the familiar.

A low growl.

'The ol' goat! Do this! Get that! Where's my paper? ME. ME. ME. Selfish, grumpy, demanding.'

'I know what you mean – my auld fella was a bastard' — the words from my mouth a bit louder than intended. 'Bossy and clingy – at the same time!'

The low growl again.

'My old man was a night owl – he couldn't sleep.'

A glazed look came over his eyes. His brow furrowed. I could see that he had drifted to a darker place. Dreadful memories looped in his brain. He spoke in a deathly voice, like an actor rehearsing for his part in a horror movie. Except, this wasn't make-believe. This was for real.

'That night, Saturday, bitch of a late shift in Shanahan's. Steak Specials night. Greasy dishes. Sticky pans. Scum everywhere. On the glasses, too. Ghastly! And last orders. Always later on a Saturday.'

'Yeah. Funny how thirsty it gets at closing time,' I said, catching the chance to order another shot and gesturing, also, for a beer chaser.

'It was pushing two-thirty when I got in. Didn't even kick off my overalls. Threw myself on the bed. Let the cool pillow do its work. Open window took the sweat. The ol' man shouted. Moaned. A low call from the next room. I groaned. Not your night, Dad. Not tonight. Jesus! Give me one straight sleep. Without the pisspot. Without the cup of tea. Anyway, he was quiet again. And I eased myself, or tumbled, into a deep sleep. In the morning, cold as ice. Face down. Hands stretched out. Y'know? Like a cross.'

'A crucifix,' I said.

'Like a crucifix, yeah. Right leg splayed out from underneath the sheet. Almost tipping the floor. Godawful. Pale skin. Pasty white. My eyes fixed on his calf. Just stared at it. A silver beacon in the darkened room. The coroner said: *Blocked artery. 100%. Hard to detect. Would've taken him in an instant!* I heard him cry out! I was too tired. Every other night I got up. Every other night. But that night, I'd just had enough. Knowing that he died all alone. Driving me crazy. Five feet away in the next room, and he died alone.'

A guilty man has a haunted look, and I knew it would take more than one bottle to quell the bile in his gut. I felt the weight of his guilt, the burden of a life wasted, the pain of loss. The more he spoke, the more I realised the stranger sitting in my chair was not so unfamiliar after all.

As he finished his tale, I said: 'Yeah. Fathers leave at the most inconvenient times.'

I ordered another whiskey, and one for the stranger. The bartender looked at me with a mix of pity and disdain. 'You've been hoggin' that stool for hours. Talkin' to yourself. Bad for business.'

He scooped up my empty glass and began to wipe the counter. Without argument, I buttoned my shirt, straightened my tie, and turned up the collar of my funeral coat to cover my neck. I dragged myself from the stool, staggered to the door, and stepped out into the cool night air. I left the stranger behind, but I knew he would be waiting for me at the bottom of my next glass.

It was Saturday night. Steak Specials night. Should've gone to work. Scouring pans. Scrubbing grease.

Keeps your mind off things.

Old Friends

'Have you spoken with Monsignor Colas recently?' Isabella asked, her fingers tracing the edges of a small frame.

'Yes, I spoke with him on the phone just yesterday, as a matter of fact,' Juliet responded with a lengthy sigh.

The sisters had dedicated their afternoon to decluttering Juliet's compact apartment, a task long overdue. Isabella, hair pinned up in a bun and dressed in faded jeans and a loose-fitting shirt, seemed to revel in the act of organisation. The floorboards, freshly waxed and polished, gleamed in the slanting light that entered through the window.

As the sun dipped below the horizon, they stopped for a tea break and to survey the fruits of their labour so far. The apartment seemed to breathe a sigh of relief, revelling in its new order and cleanliness. Juliet surveyed the room, feeling a sense of renewal, as though the act of decluttering had made space for something new to enter her life.

The photograph that Isabella held was over a decade old, portraying a youthful, radiant couple locked in an embrace.

'Have you ever thought about going back?' Isabella asked softly, stirring her tea. The question seemed to hang in the air, suspended like the steam above their cups.

'Back where?' Juliet asked, her voice tinged with confusion.

'To dancing,' Isabella replied, her eyes searching her sister's face for a reaction.

Juliet contemplated the idea, her mind drifting back to the dimly lit club and the thrum of music that had been the soundtrack of her life for a time. She remembered the sense of power she had felt, the sense of freedom and abandon as she twirled around the pole, the weight of the world seemingly left behind.

'I've thought about it, from time to time,' Juliet admitted. 'But I believe that part of my life is behind me. I've changed, and so have my desires.'

Isabella nodded, acknowledging the ebb and flow of life's passions.

As the evening deepened and the stars began to pepper the sky, the sisters shared memories of their youth, of the dreams they had once held and the paths they had chosen to walk. They spoke of love and loss, of the people who had come and gone from their lives, leaving indelible marks on their hearts.

In the quiet moments between words, Juliet felt the ghostly touch of the past, the echoes of the girl she had once been. She knew that she had come a long way since those days, shaped by the choices she had made and the people she had met.

Juliet couldn't help but reflect on that time, on Raymond – the man with the captivating eyes that had first drawn her in. She remembered the way he used to watch her from the bar, eyes never straying from her lithe form as she danced.

The club had been smoky and crowded, filled with men who all had their favourites. Juliet had learned to embrace her nudity, imagining herself as a character in a film or a member of a pop group as she clung to the shiny pole. Dancing had become second nature to her, the fact that she was completely exposed pushed to the back of her mind.

Raymond's presence, however, had stirred something within her. He had been waiting for her outside the club one night.

'May I speak with you?' he asked politely.

Juliet automatically looked to the busy street to see if any of her friends were there, and she watched the lights of the taxis, trying to find an available one. The street was deserted, and the traffic was surprisingly quite. She decided to walk at a brisk space towards her lodgings. It was only a short walk to the guest house, but she did not want the attention of this good-looking stranger.

'We don't fraternise with the customers,' Juliet said over her shoulder, as she hurried briskly away.

'I only want to talk to you,' he said.

Something in his voice halted Juliet in her tracks. It was a gentle voice, and it was almost like a plea, a reaching out for communication with another.

'Well, if you behave yourself, you can walk with me for a few minutes,' she said.

He stepped into stride with her.

'Why do you do it?' he asked.

'Do it?' she said. 'You mean why do I dance in the club?'

'Yes!' he said.

'A girl has to make a living.'

'But do you not feel...?'

'You get straight to the point, don't you? Did you ever try subtlety?'

'I'm sorry,' he said. 'Listen, my name is Raymond Colas. Will you have a coffee with me? There's a late-night place open over there.'

'And a fast mover too, I see,' laughed Juliet. She didn't feel in any danger from this young man. There was something about him that she couldn't quite put her finger on – something innocent and intriguing.

'Okay,' she said. 'A quick coffee.'

The café was nestled in a quiet corner of the city, a place that seemed untouched by the passage of time. The building was old, its brick façade weathered and worn, with ivy creeping up the walls and framing the windows like a living tapestry. As they approached, Juliet noticed the glow of warm light spilling out onto the street, casting an inviting, golden hue on the cobbled pavement.

Stepping inside, they were enveloped by the rich, comforting aroma of freshly ground coffee beans mingling with the sweet scent of pastries and the faintest hint of pipe tobacco, a reminder of a bygone era. The air was alive with the sound of quiet conversations, the gentle clink of porcelain cups against saucers, and the soft, unobtrusive melody of a jazz pianist playing in the background.

The café was filled with an eclectic mix of patrons. Elderly couples sat side by side, their hands entwined as they sipped their coffee and reminisced about days gone by. Young artists and writers huddled together in corners; their faces illuminated by the flickering candles on the tables as they passionately debated the merits of their latest ideas. And through it all, the café staff moved with practised grace, their laughter and easy banter adding to the warmth of the atmosphere.

Juliet and Raymond moved to a table near the back, bathed in the soft glow of a vintage brass chandelier. As they approached, the floorboards creaked gently beneath their feet, the sound mingling with the murmur of voices and the faint hiss of the espresso machine.

They settled into their seats, and Juliet took in the details of their surroundings. The walls were adorned with an array of paintings and photographs, each telling its own story of love, loss, and the passage of time. The furnishings were a mix of antique wooden chairs and plush velvet sofas, worn and well-loved, each piece carrying the imprint of countless memories.

Juliet was not easily shocked but what she learned next about Raymond caused her to gasp in amazement.

'I'm due to take my final vows next year,' he said. 'I don't know if I can go through with it?'

'You're a priest?'

'Did you ever try subtlety?' he laughed. 'I'm not a priest, well, not yet anyway. Even a priest must find out about the ways of the world.'

'You're a bit out of your depth in the club, then, aren't you?' said Juliet.

'I've been walking the streets these last few nights, trying to work things out. I stumbled upon the club. There was something about you that I found very attractive.'

'Now, Padre... Raymond.'

'No! I was intrigued as to how you and the other girls ended up doing what you do?'

'Raymond, you don't want to know.'

'What's your name? I didn't ask you your name.'

'My name is Juliet... you know, like Romeo and Juliet.'

In this secret haven, Juliet and Raymond exchanged confidences, the shadows of their pasts merging with the dimly lit room, creating an atmosphere of vulnerability and candour. Juliet, so used to concealing her true self, found solace in Raymond's honesty, the tension in her shoulders dissipating with each revelation he shared.

'Juliet, tell me please, tell me. I have nothing but time.'

'Padre! I am not ready for confession tonight.'

'Alright then, will you meet me tomorrow?'

'A fast mover all right!'

'Will you?'

'Tell you what,' said Juliet. 'I'm not working on Monday night. We can meet here at nine if you want?'

'Nine it is.'

'I'll see you on Monday, Raymond. Keep your thoughts pure until then.'

He laughed.

'Thanks, Juliet. I will,' he said.

Outside the window, the city continued its course, the hum of traffic and the distant peal of bells creating a subtle counterpoint to the intimate world within the café.

They lingered until the last dregs of coffee had been drained, reluctant to part ways and return to the reality that awaited them beyond the door.

Now, as Isabella prodded her about Raymond and what might have been, Juliet couldn't help but feel a pang of nostalgia.

'We worked out all of that long ago,' she said with a small smile. 'It's good to have friends.'

Big Brother

For as long as he could remember, Rory was big. Big feet. Big thighs. Big torso. Broad shoulders. Long arms. His mother used to joke that he was born half reared. Indeed, he was the heaviest baby of the two, weighing in at five and a half kilos. Even though he was the hardest to deliver – or maybe because he was the hardest to deliver – Rory's mother had a special place in her heart for him. She would never admit to having a favourite child, but there was no doubt that Rory could do no wrong in her eyes.

Rory's large frame was both his blessing and his torment. By six, his body dwarfed his older brother's, Matthew, by twice the breadth and height. Three years his senior, Matthew's disposition mirrored that of a pit-bull terrier, one that had just escaped the sting of a thistle bed. Rory could do little to placate his elder sibling; his mere existence seemed to incite Matthew's ire.

Their father, blind or indifferent to the tension, led a quiet life in the seaside town with his sons. He drove them to football practice, where, inevitably, Rory made progress through the junior ranks. In no time he was selected regularly on the senior teams. Matthew, conversely, seldom played on the first team, more often relegated to the side-lines as a spectator.

Diplomacy was a skill their father lacked. On the odd occasion when the two boys were brought to a funeral and into the pub afterwards, the father would stand his two sons side by side and ask his cronies, 'Which one is the oldest?' Rory's face would go puce. He would bend his knees slightly to reduce his height. He would take a step backwards to try to hide his bulk.

'This little chap is the runt of the litter,' a stranger would say, indicating with his finger the smaller of the two. 'You'll have to eat more for dinner to catch up with your big brother here.'

Rory's spirit would crumple, and he knew Matthew would exact a terrible retribution in private.

He bore the onslaughts with stoicism. As Matthew rained down blow after merciless blow, Rory shielded his face and wept. His pleas for mercy went unheeded. The elder brother continued his assault, driven by a need for vengeance that he could not articulate.

Rory was trapped, his very existence the source of his suffering. He could not shrink his height, alter his demeanour, or change his fate. Every perceived slight against Matthew was a weight upon Rory's shoulders.

School brought no respite. Tormented by his classmates, Matthew sought to reassert his dominance. The brothers' violent clashes became a fixture in the schoolyard, a pitiable display of sibling rivalry.

On the morning of Rory's twelfth birthday, his parents presented him with a gleaming, ten-speed racing bicycle. Its sapphire frame caught the sunlight as his father adjusted the saddle for his long legs. Rory's face was animated. Already, in his mind's eye, he was leading the Tour de France, hands in the air, pedalling to the finishing line, his yellow jersey shimmering in the heat, hordes of spectators applauding, running alongside him in adulation. With every breath, his dreams expanded.

'Be careful now, Rory,' his father cautioned. 'Don't go too fast. It's a powerful bike and you'll need time to get used to it.'

Rory mounted the saddle, eager to escape. But then, the dreaded words came.

'Matthew. Get your bike and go with Rory. Make sure that you mind him, now.'

Matthew, lurking in the shadows, emerged with a sly grin. 'Sure thing, Dad. I'll take care of him.'

Then he wheeled out his old bike, ran a little down the gravel path and expertly hopped up onto his well-worn saddle. Within a few moments, the boys were out of sight.

The unanswered question that lingered in the air after the post-mortem inquest was, 'Why was Matthew riding Rory's new bicycle when the accident happened?'

Mr Dundon, the petrol station owner, was certain of what he saw that afternoon. 'When they passed me, they were freewheeling. There's a hill outside my garage and bikes can easily pick up speed on the descent. The smaller of the two was in front, and the bigger boy was lagging. I remember thinking: "That saddle is way too high for the small lad. He'll have trouble setting his feet down on the ground when he stops!" But they were gone past in a few seconds, and I thought no more about it until I heard the awful news.'

Other locals corroborated Dundon's account. The boys were seen at various points along the picturesque coastal road to Tern Bay. The precise sequence of events leading them to Eagle's Point remains shrouded in mystery.

What is known is that Rory's new bike was discovered at the cliff's edge, its front wheel twisted and mangled. Police investigators found footprints and disturbed soil, suggesting a struggle or a rescue attempt. What is not in dispute is that Matthew's lifeless form washed ashore the following day, his body battered and bruised by the unforgiving waves and rocks.

Rory fell silent for days, his strength seemingly sapped. When rescuers found him, he babbled feverishly. In his delirium, he recounted his desperate attempt to save his brother.

'I held on to his wrist first,' he sobbed. 'He was hanging over the cliff edge. One of his hands clung to a rock, the other grasping at me. I held his wrist for ages, but it grew slippery with sweat. *Pull me up, Rory. Pull me up,* Matthew screamed. I tried, but my arms weakened. Then, I held his fingers, like we were shaking hands. I held on until one by one, they slipped away.'

Investigators noted the scratches on his wrists and forearms. They were consistent with the desperate actions of fingernails scrabbling and scraping for a crack, a crevice, a plant, or anything that would provide purchase or something to clutch on to.

Rory collapsed at the funeral as Matthew's white coffin was lowered into the ground, and he was rushed to the hospital. 'He's been through a traumatic experience,' the psychiatrist said. 'He needs time to process what has happened.'

Rory's mother stayed beside his bed. She refused to go home. 'I've lost one son. I'm not letting this boy out of my sight until he's well enough to come with me.'

The days passed. Rory tossed and turned every night, the nightmare of what happened playing repeatedly in his fevered brain. His mother was by his side, sponging the sweat from his body, soothing him with her calming words. She listened to his delirious ranting. Many people attributed his recovery to her calming influence.

Three weeks later, Rory and his mother left the hospital and returned home. Slowly, inevitably, the business of living overcame the need to grieve. Life moved on. Before Rory went back to school, his mother made him swear not to discuss the events of the tragedy with anyone. His classmates had been warned not to ask questions about the accident, and to their credit, he was left alone. The awful incident that had shattered his life was left to smoulder In his subconscious.

***

I was reminded of these events when Rory walked into my office this morning. I hadn't laid eyes on him in years. Once or twice our paths had crossed at school reunions, and I remember seeing him very drunk at a barbeque somewhere. But I had not given him, or the accident, much thought in twenty-five years.

When I looked at the stooped, dishevelled figure in front of me, I could see that he was a broken man – old before his time.

'What can I do for you, Rory?' I asked gently, after he had shuffled unsteadily to the high-backed chair. He had already declined the offer of coffee or tea, with a dismissive wave of his hand.

'I need a solicitor,' he said. 'I must confess. I want to tell you what really happened that day.'

His voice was barely louder than a whisper.

Route 309

TRIP ADVISOR

This is the road where nightmares are created. I have never been so scared as I was driving this road. No one tells you how bad it is and, once committed, you can't turn back. Do not believe your GPS – it lies. Two cars can only pass with very little room. One Jucy rental car came around a corner at high speed and almost sent us over the side into the abyss. I fail to understand how no one has ever died on this road. It should be on TV on that program 'World's Worst Roads'. I do not recommend anyone to go on this road. If you do, I hope your travel insurance is fully paid for.

We had heard and read about New Zealand's Route 309, which is a shortcut through the mountains from Pananuie towards Coromandel town. However, nothing prepared us for the terrifying journey that lay ahead.

'There's a skull and crossbones!' said Frances, pointing to a warning sign on the side of the road, as we turned onto the route.

In truth, there are warning signs everywhere to make tourists aware that this is not a road for the fainthearted. In fact, it is debatable whether Route 309 should be called a road at all. After a very short distance, the tarred surface gave way to a clay-like reddish substance and quickly after that, the road consisted of nothing more than grit and stones.

'I'll have to allow extra yardage for braking,' I said to Frances, as the wheels skidded, spewing clouds of dust and dirt on both sides of the car. The maximum speed limit was a mere 45km per hour, but it is difficult to keep a Toyota Camry to that speed. With increasing confidence, I edged the speedometer up to 60, then 65, but rapidly had to descend to 20 or 30 when cornering.

And what corners! While driving in New Zealand, I got used to 45-degree turns, and even 90-degree turns in some places. But Route 309 is fiendishly devised to give the impression that one is turning right back on oneself. For the first few kilometres of the journey, I was keeping pace with a black Volvo car, the number plate of which read END 29. Perhaps the driver was concerned for my windshield, or perhaps she just wanted me to take the lead. In any event, she slowed down and waved for me to overtake her. There was barely enough room for the two cars, and there was no ditch or edging for a car to pull over, but I drew level with her slowly, just about squeezed past her wing mirror, and then carefully pulled away, giving a thank-you wave as I headed into the next bend.

My skidding, cornering technique was being honed to a fine art and I began to take wider lines entering the bends, reasoning that there was very little possibility of meeting any on-coming traffic on this route. At the same time, I was keeping an eye in the rear-view mirror at END 29 who remained sometimes in my line of sight, but at other times appeared on a stretch of the road below me.

I suspect that I saw the white Winnebago a fraction of a second before its driver saw me. It was rounding the corner at the same time as we were turning into it from the opposite direction. There was no road in front of me because the van took up the entire space. I hit the brakes, hard. There was no screeching noise, just fumes and dust rising from the dirt track, showering the bonnet and the windscreen. Things happened in slow motion from there.

The lady driver of the lumbering Winnebago had her mouth shaped in an O, like a hungry goldfish whose owners had disappeared on a two-week vacation. The whites of her eyes were moons. Her pupils had constricted to pin pricks. Her arms were the levers of a stainless-steel nutcracker squeezing the shell of a stubborn walnut. Her knuckles glistened like ice caps. The steering wheel winced in her vice-like grip.

And all the time, the enormous van wobbled and slid forward. Our car still had not halted and we were skidding slowly towards our doom. Not only were we going to crash into the van in front, but there was every danger that the black Volvo behind us would rear-end us. How far back is it? Will END 29 come onto the scene, turning us into the meat in the sandwich?

I put my full weight on the brakes and braced myself. Before I closed my eyes, I glanced over at Frances. Her face was a portrait of pure terror. Her hands clawed at the dashboard, and her knees dug into the casing of the glove compartment.

And then, there was silence!

You couldn't squeeze an anorexic spider in the space that remained between the bumpers of the two vehicles. We had not collided. Some miracles of gravity, or decreasing velocity, had kept us apart. Just then, END 29 trundled to a halt a few centimetres from our boot.

There was a collective inhalation of deep breaths. Eventually, END 29 reversed and I pulled backwards away from the Winnebago. After much squirming and manoeuvring, the lady driving this enormous white vehicle managed to squeeze it past our Toyota, but before she pulled away, she mouthed a relieved 'Thank you!' to me or to God. She drove off. The image of her ashen face and startled eyes burned in my brain. Like Banquo's ghost, they reappear when I least expect them.

We travelled at less than 30km per hour for the remainder of the journey, and pulled in for a long black at the first roadside café that we met on the way to Coromandel. Needless to say, we stuck to the longer, main route on the way home, and we did not meet END 29 again.

The Golden Couple

News of Helen's death came as a total shock to me. When her neighbour phoned, I simply could not believe it. I rang my wife immediately.

'Jane, I've some terrible news. It's Helen McGlennon.'

'What?' said Jane.

'There's no easy way to say this. She's dead.'

'That's impossible! That couldn't be! What happened to her?'

'I don't know,' I replied. 'I couldn't get any information.'

Only a fortnight ago, we had enjoyed a delightful evening at the McGlennon residence. 'The Golden Couple' had outdone themselves once more as hosts. Ray's spaghetti Bolognese was even more delectable than usual. Wine flowed, conversations were lively, and Helen seemed vibrant, content, and healthy. I recall she wore the colourful silk scarf Ray had brought back from his recent trip to South Africa. She adored Ray; her eyes followed him constantly when they were together, and she watched the space at the door when he left the room. Ray was the family's chef whenever he was home. As a specialist surgeon with Médecins Sans Frontier, his work took him around the globe. Helen stayed at home, caring for their two teenage children who were devoted to their father.

Jane and I felt honoured to be their friends. Everything about them was extraordinary. Stories of foreign adventures and heroic deeds ensured the conversation never flagged. Ray and Helen's warmth was legendary among their vast circle of friends.

I was the vet in the village, and Jane worked in a solicitor's office in town. My introduction to the family was through Shep, the McGlennon collie, and our shared passion for golf. We formed a foursome, playing midweek and on weekends, depending on Ray's schedule. His work took him away for weeks at a time. I sometimes wondered if that was what kept his relationship with Helen – indeed, with all his friends – so fresh and vibrant.

We arrived at the church for the removal with more questions than answers. I had probed the neighbours to find out what caused Helen's death. Was it cancer that she kept hidden from us? Was it a brain tumour? An accident? A fall? Nobody appeared to have any information. If they had, they were not sharing it.

The churchyard was thronged with mourners, and we arrived just as the funeral cortege was pulling in. Ray and his two children stepped out from a dark Mercedes. He greeted various sympathisers before spotting me and approaching.

'I'm so sorry for your troubled,' I said, extending my hand.

'Thank you both for coming,' Ray replied. 'I wasn't sure if you would.'

'Of course,' Jane and I said in unison. 'Why wouldn't we be here? If there's anything we can do...? Anything at all...?'

'Well,' Ray said, 'I'd like you both to join us at the house afterward.'

'Oh, Ray, we don't want to impose. The house will be filled with your family and relations. You'll have enough to do without having us there.'

'No,' Ray insisted. 'I want you to come. Please promise me you'll be there.'

'Sure, Ray. No problem. We'll be there after the service.'

The anxious look on Ray's face vanished. He smiled gratefully and thanked us again before re-joining his family.

'What was that about?' Jane asked me.

'I'm not sure,' I replied, feeling uneasy. 'There's something peculiar going on here. Has anyone told you anything about Helen's death?'

'No,' she said. 'I thought I heard someone saying that they had difficulty recovering the body.'

'Recovering the body?'

'That's what I thought I heard.'

During the ceremony, the priest spoke of the tragic loss and described Helen as an exemplary wife, mother, neighbour, and friend. Her passion for life was well-known, he said and her love for her family meant everything. How such a tragedy occurred was a mystery. Only God, all-knowing and all-powerful, could understand such an event. All we can do is offer our condolences to her husband, children, and family, he concluded. May she rest in peace.

From snippets of conversation around the church, we gathered that Helen had drowned. Her body had been recovered from the Arden River after being missing for two days. What led her to the river? Was it a tragic accident or something more sinister? No one could fathom how Helen could have reached such a state of despair. Nobody dared to utter the word 'suicide,' let alone associate it with one half of the Golden Couple.

Upon arriving at the McGlennon's house, we were surprised by the scarcity of cars and people. We had expected a crowded gathering of friends, family, and well-wishers. Instead, only two cars sat in the driveway. Ray welcomed us at the door.

'I'm so glad you could make it,' he said, guiding us into the living room. An elderly couple dressed in dark clothing rose from the couch as we entered.

'Meet Helen's father, Jack, and her mother, Rita,' Ray introduced.

After exchanging formal condolences, Ray switched to host mode. 'What would you like to drink? Whiskey? Wine?'

With Ray out of the room, we struggled to make small talk with the grieving parents. There were photos of Helen on the mantelpiece: Helen golfing, Helen with her children. None of Helen and Ray together.

What do you say to the parents of a woman who has taken her own life? To her husband? I was at a loss for words. Luckily, Jane was used to making small talk and she kept up a steady stream of conversation, telling the parents about Helen's golfing exploits, how they used to play bridge together, and what a wonderful cook she was.

Helen's parents barely spoke, on the verge of tears. Jack stared into his whiskey glass and didn't acknowledge Ray when he refilled it.

I found the tension unbearable, so after finishing my drink, I announced it was time for us to leave as I had animals to attend to that evening.

'It was kind of you to come,' Ray said solemnly. 'Helen would have appreciated it.'

We shook hands, embraced, and offered to help in any way during these difficult days. On the way home, we tried to piece together what had transpired. We sensed the terrible atmosphere in the living room. Helen's parents were understandably distraught and mourning, but their silence and sullenness bordered on hostility toward Ray. They were hardly civil with us.

The next day, we attended the funeral and burial. This time, we did not return to the house afterward. I was eager to get back to my clinic. A six-year-old Labrador with a fractured pelvis was close to giving birth to a large litter of pups. Without my assistance, things could get extremely complicated.

My receptionist was skilled at arranging appointments and ensuring the animals were well cared for. She was also a gossip. Jane called her 'Nosey Nora.'

'How was the funeral?' Nora asked when I arrived.

'Busy and crowded,' I said.

'Did you talk to Ray?' she inquired. 'Just a few words of sympathy. He had his hands full, as you can imagine.'

'Indeed,' said Nora. 'Hands full, indeed.'

I decided not to ask her what she meant until after I had investigated the mum-in-waiting. A quick examination told me that the pups would not be born until later in the evening. I made sure she was fed and watered. Then, I made a cup of coffee and sidled out to the reception area.

'What can you tell me about Helen's death?' I asked Nora. 'What have you heard?'

'You know me, Mr. Devoy, I hear bits and pieces. But I can't be certain, and I don't want to spread malicious rumours.'

I raised an eyebrow.

'Malicious?'

'Well, it's not really for me to say,' Nora continued.

'Just give me some idea of what's being said. There's no harm in that.'

Nora didn't need further prompting.

'It must have been shocking for her to receive that phone call from Paris.'

'Paris?' I said.

'Oh yes, Paris. If it wasn't for the local police following up, we might never have heard about it at all.'

'Heard about what?'

I was beginning to lose patience.

'Yer man, Ray. And the accident.'

'Accident? Nora, in plain English, could you tell me what you know?'

'Ray had a car crash in Paris. I believe the car was a write-off, but remarkably, he only suffered cuts and bruises. He did get a bump in the head and he was unconscious for a while. That's what did for him.'

'What do you mean?'

'If he hadn't been unconscious, maybe he would have prevented the phone call.'

'The phone call?'

'Yes. A female officer phoned Helen to inform her about the crash. She got her number from Ray's phone. She told Helen that her brother had been in an accident.'

'Her brother?' I asked.

'Helen explained that she was Ray's wife. The officer said that that couldn't be true because his wife was with him in the car.'

'His wife?' I gasped.

'The woman was in intensive care after the accident,' said Nora. 'I wonder if she survived?'

We lapsed into a silence that was laden with unspoken thoughts and emotions.

'It seems Ray was playing offside, away from home,' said Nora after a few moments. 'Nobody knew. If it weren't for the car crash, no one would ever have found out.'

'Thanks, Nora,' I said. 'You can leave now. I'll stay and look after the mum-to-be and her pups. I'll see you tomorrow.'

Nora was delighted to head home early. I closed the window shutters and took my coffee into the clinic.

'The Golden Couple,' I said to myself. 'The Golden Couple. Poor Helen. Does one ever know?'

Western Melody Surprise

Sally sped across the Salmon Weir Bridge, her plastic raincoat a cape billowing behind her. She disregarded the icy flurries that whipped around her and the splashes from passing cars. The narrow footpath over the bridge was clogged with strolling Christmas shoppers.

Unperturbed, she focused on her task. The first puzzle was solved, and the second clue had illuminated her path forward.

Grasping tightly to the second envelope in her raincoat pocket, she questioned herself. Was her answer correct? No time to be wrong. Woodquay beckoned. Less than a minute away. The pedestrian lights hindered her stride momentarily, but she dashed across the road without hesitation.

Sally's day began at a leisurely pace, despite a restless night. A clue from the crossword had her tossing and turning before she finally conceded defeat:

Kneels excited over bone from duck found in archaeological site.

In the morning, the answer seemed painfully simple. 'T-bone!' she exclaimed, splattering toothpaste all over the mirror. 'And duck also means zero!'

With pen in hand, she filled in the eight-letter answer. 'Kneels,' combined with 't' and 'o' provided the solution to the anagram.

S-K-E-L-E-T-O-N.

She imagined Jack's voice sharing in her excitement. 'Atta gal, Sal! Atta gal!' Her chest tightened with the recollection. She sighed.

Attractive and in her mid-fifties, Sally was just getting used to her new hairstyle—a shiny chestnut bob. Carefully applied makeup concealed her pale face and the dark circles that had marred her appearance since Jack's death.

She had finally allowed herself to wear brighter clothes again. It was a special day—the university's traditional free afternoon for Christmas shopping. Her fuchsia-coloured tunic and patterned scarf contrasted sharply with the dark attire that had become her norm, contributing to her light-hearted mood. She was putting the final touches to her lip gloss when she heard the snap of the letterbox.

Swiftly, she poured water into her instant coffee and lavished a heap of coarse-cut, orange marmalade over two slices of thickly buttered toast.

Once she had donned her raincoat, she smiled at her reflection in the hall mirror, nodding approvingly. As she opened the front door, the heel of her ankle boot skidded on a white envelope. Scooping it up and shoving it into her handbag, she left.

She remembered the letter again at lunchtime. Her friend, Cheryl, was a crossword buff, and they had slipped into a ritual of completing the Simplex over coffee and a sandwich, leaving the cryptic crossword for the evenings. Their sons had gone to school together and were close friends. But all that changed when Barry, Sally's son, left abruptly after an explosive argument. Sally could barely recall the incident that caused the row. But neither Barry nor his father could put the pin back in the grenade. Barry went on a backpacking holiday to Southeast Asia. He never returned. Not even for the funeral. He hardly ever wrote. Sally's heart was sundered.

Putting aside the crossword, she retrieved the envelope from her bag.

Cheryl watched the expression on her friend's face change to an open-mouthed stare. 'What is it, Sal? What's the matter?'

'I'm sorry, Cher, I have to go. I'll call you later.'

Sally reached Woodquay. She sheltered in the doorway of McSwiggan's restaurant and pulled her plastic raincoat up over her head. Then, she unfurled the second letter from her fist.

Sounds like Karl
Is a little Italian charlatan
In a timber dock.

The timber dock was none other than Woodquay, she was certain. A little Italian charlatan – could it signify an Italian barbershop, or perhaps something else distinctly Italian? With a sense of intrigue, she crossed over to The Lough Inn, and as her eyes gleamed, she saw, on the corner of St Anthony's Place, snugly nestled beside a dwelling house, a small café and bakery, Ciarlantini Delizie Italiane.

Sally crossed the street, shrugged off her plastic raincoat, and went into the café.

Within, the atmosphere was warm and bustling. She positioned herself upon a high stool facing the front window, where she could observe her own reflection and the other diners simultaneously. A dark-eyed waitress with a profusion of black curls set to wiping the counter with a damp cloth.

'Americano, in a take-away cup,' Sally requested. She might have to move quickly. Somewhere in this establishment, the third clue awaited discovery.

She retrieved the first envelope from her handbag and examined it once more.

For unto us a Child is born,
unto us a Son is given (Isaiah 9:6)
Follow the clues until they end.
Seek and find a true amend.

From the university, she had dashed straight to the Cathedral, spurred on by the first clue:

Once a place of torment
Now a house of prayer
Go to where it all began.
We'll light a candle there.

Sally knew that the Cathedral was built on the site of Old Galway Gaol. A plaque in the carpark commemorated the last hanging that took place there in 1902.

The meaning of the third line of the clue eluded her until she saw the signs to 'Visit the Christmas Crib'.

She lit a candle and waited. After a few minutes, she investigated the Crib further. She wondered if she would have to climb over the altar rail and lift the statues.

The line from Isaiah 9:6 played over and over in her head. Sally was a member of Western Medley Choir and Handel's *Messiah* was the heart of their repertoire.

Her mind focussed on the last line of the clue.

Of course! The candles! Facing the altar were two votive candle racks, each with a drawer underneath. Discretely, she rummaged her fingers through the candles in the first drawer. Nothing. But she was rewarded at the second drawer. Buried underneath the candles, invisible to the unsuspecting eye, was a white envelope. Written on the front of the envelope was Clue Number 2. This had led her to the café in Woodquay.

In the reflection of the front window, she began to study the customers. Did she recognise anyone from the Cathedral? Had she been followed here?

A family sat at the table directly behind her. The two children were sipping smoothies from tall colourful glasses. Their parents were studiously ignoring each other. An Asian girl was writing in her jotter while sipping a latte. Nobody paid any attention to Sally.

For the next few minutes, she observed people coming and going. Each cold blast of air brought another stranger.

She decided to investigate the other nooks and crannies that had been invisible from her vantage point. When she returned to her seat a few minutes later, she was surprised to find a yellow Post-it note stuck to the side of her cup.

'That's strange,' she muttered. She saw the familiar lettering.

Clue 3
Sounds like a Swedish band member
became Christian
to re-enter this Christmas store.
The password is 'Messiah'!

Sally frowned. Who had placed the message there? Furtively, she looked around. Nothing out of the ordinary. She settled down to apply herself to the clue.

A 'Swedish band' brought ABBA to mind. One of the members was named Björn. 'A born-again Christian.' Of course! The Born Christmas Store near Woodquay in Newtownsmith.

'They were left here this morning,' the haughty woman in the Born uniform told her. 'Before I came on duty. I didn't see who delivered them. It's highly irregular, you know. I'm supposed to ask for a code word.'

'*Messiah!*' Sally said.

Each new clue had led Sally to different parts of the city. She phoned Cheryl on several occasions, seeking help with the answers. The chirpy answering machine kicked in each time:

'Hi! This is Cheryl's fridge. Please speak slowly, and I'll stick your message to myself with one of these magnets.'

Now, she was in the Park House Hotel in Forster Street.

Finally, an abode on a greenfield site within view of a holy patron. A fine mess to get into.

Once she remembered that St Patrick's Church was across the street from the hotel, and that a 'mess' was also the name for a canteen, the clue had given up its secrets.

Paul, the tall, polite waiter who had attended Jack's funeral and who always addressed her formally, showed her to a table.

'A gin and tonic, Mrs Cronin?' he asked.

'Thank you, Paul,' she said.

Her mind was absorbed by the events of the day. The package from Born contained a small, ornamental crib. Judy Greene's Pottery also had an envelope ready for her. Once she announced the password, to Sally's surprise, she was presented with a pair of beautiful pendant earrings with a fuchsia motif. When she had resolved the riddle of the jewellers where the first Claddagh Ring had been crafted, she had received a small gift box containing a gold Claddagh pendant.

A crash course in repair on Shop Street.

The Body Shop had yielded a gift basket of perfume and cinnamon scented bathroom treats. Even the Christmas market in Eyre Square had offered up treasures of confectionery and ornaments, once she had solved the clues.

A day full of surprises. And mystery.

Paul reappeared with her drink. His smile had been replaced by a perplexed expression and he knit his eyebrows.

'I'm very sorry, Mrs Cronin, but I've been told that this table is required for a party who made a reservation earlier. Would you mind terribly if I asked you to move?'

'Not in the slightest, Paul,' said Sally and she followed him dutifully through the restaurant towards a door in a brightly lit annex. This corner of the hotel was new to her.

'I think you will find that you will be more comfortable here,' he said.

'Thank you, Paul,' she said with a smile, as he held the door open for her.

The room into which Sally stepped was pitch-black. She was about to turn to ask Paul to turn on the lights when the darkness exploded into light and a roar of voices shouted in unison:

'SURPRISE!'

Sally nearly stumbled with the shock! People were calling her name, clapping, cheering and singing. Adjusting her eyes to the brightness, she began to recognise some of the singers from Western Medley. A group of classical musicians accompanied them. She felt lost for words.

Luckily, Paul was on hand to support her and to lead her through the crowd to a table at the top of the room. Cheryl came towards her. She was wearing a chic pair of black, tapered pants with a white blouse, brightened by a red carnation.

'What's the occasion, Cher? What's going on?' Sally pleaded. 'Did you organise all of this?'

'Oh, Sal, Sal. I'm so happy for you. You deserve the best possible Christmas.'

At that moment, a hush descended on the gathering. People began to move to the sides of the room. An aisle was created leading from the entrance door to the top table. A tall, bearded young man entered and strode confidently towards Sally.

She gasped and stood with her arms spread wide in greeting.

He leaned over to hug her.

'Mum,' he said.

'Barry,' she said, unable to say any more.

'Mum, I have some good news for you.'

Sally's eyes filled with tears. An Asian girl appeared at the door. She carried an infant. Sally remembered the girl from the café.

The musicians struck up and the Western Medley Choir began singing: 'For unto us a Child is Born'.

'Oh, Barry,' Sally cried. 'My beautiful boy.'

He smiled.

'Yes, Mum. *Unto us a Son is Given.*'

They hugged each other for a long time.

Then, he whispered:

'We named him Jack.'

A Sister's Duty

Clutching her small, travel suitcase, Julie stepped out into the dark street. The clatter of her high heels was the only sound to be heard as she hurried to catch the first airport bus. It was four in the morning and the cold, bracing air prompted her to turn up the collar of her black overcoat. Her hat covered her unwashed hair and provided her with a ceiling against the dark skies. It was a soft-brimmed, grey hat; she thought it was practical and stylish. It would match her outfit for the funeral. Imagine! Thinking about what she was going to wear, rather than the grisly task in hand.

The bus departed on time. There were three other passengers; an elderly couple who shared a large suitcase, and a teenage girl with her worldly possessions in a backpack. Julie picked a seat at the back. The last thing she needed was conversation. She envied them, heading for the airport, no doubt to catch a flight to distant parts. Julie's journey was not so exotic. In fact, it was a grim task. The worst her sister had ever given to her.

The phone call in the early hours spelled disaster. Nobody phoned at two o'clock in the morning with good news. Bill never stirred. Julie raced downstairs to the hallstand in her nightdress. She grabbed the phone before the ringing stopped.

Veronica's voice quivering.

'It's Jonathon,' she said, between sobs. 'My darling, Jonathon.'

The image of a handsome, seventeen-year-old boy, tall and athletic, came to Julie's mind. Veronica's eldest.

A sudden, cold draught in the hallway made Julie shiver. She gripped the receiver tightly to her ear with both hands.

'What about Jonathon?' she asked.

'Something dreadful has happened. Dreadful.'

'Veronica, it's two o'clock in the morning.'

'For once in your life, can you listen?'

The cutting tone. Even during tragedy, she had to domineer. Veronica had married Jim, well-to-do businessman with a seat on the Council. She had moved up in the world. Detached house in the country. Private schools for her children. Julie still lived on the old housing estate. Her Bill was a shopkeeper. A good father and a loving husband. But, a shopkeeper?

'Veronica, tell me, tell me.'

'It's dreadful. I can't even imagine it.'

'For god's sake, have you been drinking?'

Jim & Veronic were well named. The joke was that Jim had 'Schweppes' her off her feet! They were never too far away from some celebration or other.

'Have *I* been drinking? What do you mean, have I been drinking? Tonight, of all nights. Why tonight, of all nights?'

'Veronica! You'd better start making sense or I'll...'

'Oh, for Christ's sake! Can you just shut up and listen? Spare me the lecture.'

'Veronica, I'm going to hang up now.'

'Don't you fucking try. He's missing. My Jonathon is missing.'

Julie felt her knees go weak. She reached for the hallstand to steady herself. The tearful sobbing gave way to another sound. A primordial wail. The anguished cry of a trapped animal.

'Veronica. Veronica. Listen to me. Tell me what you know.'

'Mis-, mis-, missing, they said,' came the stammered response.

'Who said?'

'Father Mul-, Mulryan.'

Father Mulryan, sophisticated, pompous, portly. Beloved of the toffee-nosed set and principal of the school. The look he gave to Julie when she accompanied Veronica to the Entrance interview.

'They were camping out ...'

'Camping out?' Julie said. 'Where were they?'

'Don't be asking me for details. Jonathon was in Annaghmore. A scouts' jamboree.'

'And what did Father Mulryan say?'

The sound of liquid being poured into a glass. Veronica slurping.

'Jonathon is missing. A night-time picnic. A moonlight swim.'

'Oh my god,' said Julie. The receiver dropped from her hands, and she slumped to the floor in the hallway.

'Bill!' she shrieked. 'Oh Bill, come down here.'

The bus pulled in at the station in Ballinasloe. Five or six passengers boarded, and quickly stored away their luggage. In a matter of minutes, the bus squeezed its way out of the station and turned towards the streaks of dawn that caressed the sky over the Dublin road.

Julie remembered the shock. It was just impossible to imagine that Jonathon would never again stride into her house and give her a big hug.

'How's Auntie Julie? My favourite auntie in the whole world!'

Such innocence. Such a sweet boy.

Bill had rescued her from the floor and insisted on making tea in the kitchen. The next hour was spent in a haze of hurried arrangements. The pot of fresh tea lay untouched on the kitchen table. How could Bill possibly close the shop? Why couldn't Veronica and Jim go themselves? Why had she to ask her little sister to do everything?

But they both knew. Julie was the responsible one. Bill could take care of the children. He would make preparations for when the time came to join his wife. Bill was dependable.

They had rung the guards. The nice, young Sergeant had been more than helpful. It was him who suggested getting the Airport bus. In Athlone, the gardai would meet her and bring her to Annaghmore.

The journey to Annaghmore Lough was going to be tough, especially as she had to travel alone. Why was it that, in times of crisis, she always ended up alone? Bill couldn't afford to close the shop mid-week. He would join her at the weekend if the body had not been found beforehand.

The Sergeant had warned her that it could take the Garda Sub Aqua Divers three or four days to recover a drowning victim. Annaghmore Lough has undercurrents, and these tend to spiral towards the reeds below. The reeds would add considerably to the difficulty in locating the cadaver. Cadaver was the word he used. He tried to prepare her for the ordeal that lay ahead. As gently as he could, he spoke to her about how a body gets discoloured and bloated. There was no easy way to tell her about the destructive nature of pike, eels and other lake-water life.

Lake-water life. Lake-water death. Ironic, she thought. A rotting corpse could provide life for other creatures. Jonathon. A rotting corpse. A cadaver. A bloated body. The spark of life extinguished. For what?

The bus reached the outskirts of Athlone. The station was close now. Soon, this leg of her journey would be over.

Her thoughts returned to the moonlit picnic. She could picture Jonathon, goaded on by the other boys. 'I bet you couldn't swim across the lake.'

A moment of bravado. A challenge. Poor Jonathon. Never one to resist. A reckless streak.

'Swim across the lake? Just watch me!'

Oh, Jonathon. His white teeth glowing in the moonlight. His rippling muscles as he discarded his t-shirt. His shock of blond hair carelessly brushed out of his eyes. Those eyes. Dancing with excitement. Capable of anything. Superman. A god.

Now, at the bottom of the lake with fish, slugs and snails feeding off him.

Julie could see the lights of the bus station in the distance.

Shivers crawled down her spine at the thought of poor Jonathon entangled in the reeds.

She barely noticed the young guard helping her down from the bus and leading her to the squad car. The journey was a blur and conversation was kept to a minimum. By the time they reached the guesthouse, the early streaks of dawn had given way to a light blue sky. Mrs Brady sympathised with Julie, showed her to her room and put the kettle on for tea.

The church bell pealed its seven o'clock wake-up call. The sleepy village stirred to life as the squad car pulled away from the guesthouse to bring her to the lake.

Putting Shakespeare in the Shade

All my days, I have been a creature of books. Once, I was commissioned to aid a scholarly institution in the task of devising reading materials for pupils throughout the European educational system. To achieve this, I had to select various specimens of esteemed literature and design a series of questions to discern the students' responses and comprehension of the texts.

I chose to include several eminent authors from the United States: Ernest Hemingway; F. Scott Fitzgerald; Robert Frost; Raymond Carver; Philip Roth; and John Irving.

I then chose a selection of cherished British writers: Chaucer; Shakespeare; Wordsworth; Keats; T.S. Eliot; and Philip Larkin.

My assemblage of European authors encompassed Cervantes; Guy de Maupassant; Jean-Paul Sartre; Heinrich Böll; Franz Kafka; and Günter Grass.

My selection would not be complete without the great Irish authors: James Joyce; George Bernard Shaw; Samuel Beckett; Seamus Heaney; Maeve Binchy; and Roddy Doyle.

An eclectic congregation, one must concur.

Having made my selections, I revisited the instructions, only to discover I was one item shy of the requisite amount. I contemplated a fresh expedition through the volumes of world literature lining my shelves. But time was the enemy. I elected to pursue a more expedient course. In years past, I had authored a piece intended for a younger audience, and I surmised it might be apt. Conveniently, I had already formulated a complementary series of probing questions akin to those needed for the European endeavour.

With minimal further deliberation, I included my own piece, thought no more about it, and assumed that no one would notice the cuckoo in the nest, the humble interloper among the world's finest, the minion among the recognised greats.

Several weeks later, imagine my astonishment upon receiving a missive from my European employers. They expressed gratitude for a task well-executed and praised my selections. However, they noted that other publishers and academics had been assigned identical undertakings. A single selection per individual was permitted.

In the case of the literary assemblage I had compiled, they rejected Shakespeare, Shaw, and Sartre; Hemingway, Heaney, and Kafka were cast aside; in truth, they discarded all but my own contribution.

'Who is this gifted wordsmith?' the adjudicators inquired. 'He seems to have struck a most fitting chord. His ruminations are deemed quite appropriate; his queries and explorations are exemplary. Indeed, it is the most pertinent article of the entire collection.'

Elated?

I found myself at a loss for words.

Me? A colossus of literature? Maybe not. Perhaps fortune favoured me, and I merely produced a well-crafted piece at the right time, in the right place. Nevertheless, it makes a good after-dinner story: *How I put Shakespeare into the shade!*

And the article that was accepted? It was entitled *Two Party Pieces*. Here it is.

Rivers have forever enthralled me. My most cherished recollections are of summer holidays spent on my Uncle John's farm. As soon as I arrived, I would eagerly cross the fields, armed with my notebook and pen, to reach my favoured sanctuary. The boundless expanse of farmland, the azure heavens, the ceaseless brilliance of the sun (for the sun never ceased to shine in those days!) inspired my earliest scribblings – the poems of my youth.

My worldly experience was scarce, but nature, resplendent in its summer finery, supplied the raw material for crafting verse. The diverse activities unfolding within those pastoral fields, the lush shrubs, and wildflowers, filled my head and my pen with vivid depictions of the mystical world beneath the open sky.

My preferred location was by the river. With ears as taut as antennae, I would attune myself to the splosh and splash of water babbling over stones, and the more delicate puttering sound of the liquid finding its way across pebbles. Now and again, a brown trout would leap into the air, a taut spring seeking ephemeral insects. It would pirouette mid-flight, its body a graceful arc, before descending with the gentlest of plops back into the hidden recesses of the riverbed. The incessant motion of the water, murmuring and gushing, invigorated me.

Even during sweltering summers, when the river dwindled to a mere stream, it still unveiled its mysteries. I marvelled at how a river so deep and powerful during the rains could, so swiftly, be reduced to a mere rivulet. On one such occasion, a sizeable eel found itself ensnared in a pond on the riverbed, swimming in ever-shrinking circles. Witnessing my distress, Uncle John rescued the eel, scooping it up in a bucket and releasing it farther upstream.

One evening, after the day's farm work had been completed, the hay stored and the cows milked, Uncle John accompanied me to the river. Along the way, he cut down two sally rods, produced some horse-tail hair from his pocket, and effortlessly fashioned two fishing rods, never breaking his stride. I recall the squelching sound of his boots as he walked, the sweet scent of tobacco wafting from his pipe, and the dexterity of his fingers as they twisted the silken threads into slick nooses atop each rod. The horsehair, black and fine and wiry, was as pliable as a feather yet stronger than any chain.

Uncle John demonstrated how to slide the noose beneath the trout, tickle its belly, and lull it into a slumber. Then, with a flick of the wrist, snare the trout in the noose and, in the same movement, toss it into the air and onto the riverbank.

When I composed my childish nature poems, the river figured prominently in most of them. My vocabulary was limited; 'evaporate' was an impressive term for me; 'gurgled' and 'sparkling' were overused; and the water was always in 'constant motion' or in 'torrents.'

Imagine, then, how my eyes were opened, and my vocabulary expanded as I began to take an interest in English literature. Our exceptional English teacher altered my world when he introduced me to the magical phrases employed by Samuel Coleridge in *Kubla Khan*.

> *In Xanadu did Kubla Khan*
> *A stately pleasure-dome decree:*
> *Where Alph, the sacred river, ran*
> *Through caverns measureless to man*
> *Down to a sunless sea.*

It may have been penned in an opium-induced delirium, but none can dispute that the depiction of the sacred river is a masterpiece of linguistic dexterity. Many of us can recite the opening lines, but the true descriptive prowess and potency are reserved for the sacred river, which churns with 'ceaseless turmoil seething' before 'meandering with a mazy motion' and finally sinking 'in tumult to a lifeless ocean.'

> *And from this chasm, with ceaseless turmoil*
> *seething,*
> *As if this earth in fast thick pants were*
> *breathing,*
> *A mighty fountain momently was forced:*
> *Amid whose swift half-intermitted burst*
> *Huge fragments vaulted like rebounding hail,*
> *Or chaffy grain beneath the thresher's flail:*
> *And mid these dancing rocks at once and ever*

It flung up momently the sacred river.
Five miles meandering with a mazy motion
Through wood and dale the sacred river ran,
Then reached the caverns measureless to man,
And sank in tumult to a lifeless ocean;
And 'mid this tumult Kubla heard from far
Ancestral voices prophesying war!

A finer description of a river could not be found. So captivated was I by this poem that I committed it to memory. To this day, I can recite every line. It has served me well as my party piece.

As people grow older, they form opinions and believe steadfastly in certain unassailable truths. They are hesitant to change what they know to be fact. They become set in their ways. I was afflicted with this obstinacy. The older I grew, the more resolute I became in dismissing any notion that a superior arrangement of words to describe a river could exist or be conceived. In my estimation, Samuel Taylor Coleridge had monopolised the market for depicting rustic running water.

Children and grandchildren entered my life. One evening, I found myself needing to entertain a twelve-year-old beset by the malaise of his generation—an inability to focus on anything other than a television set, a PlayStation, or an electronic device displaying moving images.

From my vantage point as a Literary Fossil, I resolved to encourage the child to develop an appreciation for the world of books. Searching the shelves in my daughter's kitchen, I spotted a worn copy of *The Wind in the Willows*, nestled between *Jamie's 15-minute Meals* and *Diet for a Small Planet* by Frances Moore Lappé. Undoubtedly, all three books were bestsellers, but hardly the stuff of classical literature.

Kenneth Grahame first published his tale of anthropomorphic riverbank animals in 1908. Mole, Rat, Toad, and Badger have delighted children of all ages for more than a century. How had they eluded me? I began to read the story to my inattentive progeny. To my astonishment, I encountered a passage in the opening section that made my jaw drop. In an instant, I realised that *Kubla Khan's* exalted status as the undisputed champion of river descriptions was no more. As my grandchild yawned on my lap, I read the following passage:

He thought his happiness was complete when, as he meandered aimlessly along, suddenly he stood by the edge of a full-fed river. Never in his life had he seen a river before – this sleek, sinuous, full-bodied animal, chasing and chuckling, gripping things with a gurgle and leaving them with a laugh, to fling itself on fresh playmates that shook themselves free, and were caught and held again. All was a-shake and a-shiver – glints and gleams and sparkles, rustle and swirl, chatter and bubble. The Mole was bewitched, entranced, fascinated. By the side of the river he trotted as one trots, when very small, by the side of a man who holds one spellbound by exciting stories; and when tired at last, he sat on the bank, while the river still chattered on to him, a babbling procession of the best stories in the world, sent from the heart of the earth to be told at last to the insatiable sea.

Coleridge had been dethroned, not by a fellow giant of classical literature, but by the vivid pictorial descriptive powers of a children's book author! The irony was not lost on this priggish bibliophile. Suitably chastened, I expanded my repertoire to include another party piece.

And so, my life took an unforeseen turn, one that demonstrated to me the importance of remaining open to the beauty and wisdom found in the most unexpected places. No longer did I cling to the steadfast belief that only the greats of literature could dazzle with their descriptions and insights.

In the years that followed, I continued to explore new works and authors, allowing my appreciation for the written word to flourish. I found enchantment in the simplest of children's stories and uncovered depth in modern literary works. My once-narrow perspective had broadened, and with it, so too did my ability to engage with others about literature.

Now, when I attend gatherings or find myself in the company of fellow literary enthusiasts, I am armed not only with my beloved *Kubla Khan* but also with the charming description of the river from *The Wind in the Willows*. In sharing these party pieces, I am reminded of my own journey and the lesson I learned: that the richness of language and the power of storytelling can be found in the most surprising of places, and that one should never cease to explore the vast world of literature, lest we miss the gems hidden within.

An Irish Goodbye

You know that moment. The waitress has taken the orders. The wine hasn't yet arrived. The pre-dinner introductions have lurched into an awkward silence. Everyone is waiting for a cue, a conversation opener, a joke, a *bon mot*, an item of news that will prime the pump to get the chatter started up again. Once the flow begins, the evening's chit-chat will trundle on under its own steam without further need of prompting or cajoling.

Sis had waited for this precise moment. It was the perfect time to announce the birth of the new arrival. She had wrapped it carefully in tissue and secreted it gingerly into her outer coat pocket. On her journey to the restaurant, she had patted this pocket on more than one occasion, just to assure herself that it was still there, had not fallen out, or worse... been stolen!

As her two brothers and their wives looked on, she dramatically rose from the table and announced: 'Ladies and gentlemen, hot off the press, it gives me great pleasure to present to you the first copy of *Away with the Breeze.*'

Four pairs of eyes watched in silence as Sis unveiled the paperback from its swaddling of tissues and placed it carefully on the table. Uncomfortable glances were exchanged.

The younger brother was first to speak.

'I'll tell you now, Sis, you won't be able to sell that book anywhere.'

'Why not?' she responded, aghast.

'Look at the banner on the cover: *Proof Copy – Not for Re-Sale.*'

'This is an advance proof copy, you idiot,' she stammered, but before she could say any more, the younger sister-in-law chimed in: 'You're going to get into BIG trouble over this!'

With slumped shoulders, Sis resumed her seat and stared at her.

'B-I-G trouble,' she repeated, wagging the index finger of her right hand at Sis until it was merely centimetres from her nose. A school principal cajoling a recalcitrant student.

'Why am I going to get into big trouble?' Sis whispered timidly.

'You need to get permission from the City Council before you can use their logo!'

'Oh,' Sis said.

'You can't just stick the City Council logo on the back cover, you know,' the wagging finger continued, accompanied now by a sad shaking of the head. In fact, there were two heads bowed in supplication as the older sister-in-law appeared to agree with this portent of doom. Such wrath would descend upon Sis for her moment of indiscretion! Imagine an experienced editor not knowing that she needed to get permission to use an official logo! Only the help of God could save her now.

'And look! You have used it inside as well!'

Further mortification! Like a contagious disease, a tribal 'tut-tutting', finger wagging, and serious head shaking afflicted each family member in turn. An objective onlooker could easily surmise that this wretched gathering was a funeral party, deep in the throes of mourning at the loss of a loved one.

Sis had gathered her thoughts and was about to deliver her opening rebuttal, when the elder brother said: 'I've found a spelling mistake'.

A collective intake of breath.

'A spelling mistake?' gulped Sis, her intended refutation of the illegal logo fiasco fading into a distant memory. 'But the printed books are sailing across the Irish Sea in shipping containers even as we speak!'

'I won't tell you what the mistake is so,' said the elder brother.

'Oh, put me out of my misery,' Sis sighed.

'Honour,' read the elder brother. 'That's not how you spell that word.'

'Is it not?' said Sis.

'No,' said the elder brother. 'The way to spell it is *h-o-n-o-r*.' He enunciated every letter with perfect diction, allowing a suitable pause between each, emphasising that this spelling lesson, delivered with accuracy and precision, would leave no room for misunderstanding, ambiguity or variance.

'I see,' said Sis. 'Even though *honor* is the American spelling?'

Her brother did not respond.

She took the book back, wrapped it in its tissue and placed it carefully in her outer pocket.

'Did anyone see the wine waiter?' she asked. 'I know that this restaurant has a fine reputation for excellent, lesser-known French reds. We really ought to give them a whirl.'

She rose from her seat.

'If you give me a minute, I'll find the waiter,' she said. 'I'm sure we can have a round of drinks brought down while we're waiting for the food.'

With that, she strode toward the entrance, her footsteps echoing through the silence she left behind. The cool night air embraced her as she stepped out, disappearing into the darkness, leaving the remnants of the evening behind her— an Irish departure, as swift and sudden as the breeze.

Seeking Solitude

With a light heart, Alicja Kowalski set off from the village on what was to be the final walk of her short life. Stopping at the signpost over the bridge to take a selfie, she flicked her long brown hair out of her eyes. She pinched her cheeks, as her mother had taught her, to give herself a little colour. When she smiled, she revealed fixed teeth braces on her upper row. *Only another month to go before I can dump them forever*, she sighed, her tongue rubbing over the bumpy wire. She took two selfies. In one, she smiled broadly at her camera making sure to keep the words *Fáilte go Uachtar Árd* firmly in focus. In the other, she tousled her hair, pulled a face, stuck her tongue out mischievously and made a V sign with two raised fingers.

The little village of Oughterard had exceeded her expectations. It seemed to Alicja that she had gone back in time. The sleepy Owenriff River yawned its way from the brown Connemara hills to Lough Corrib, keeping to a slow meandering rhythm. The locals had adapted to this tempo, going about their day-to-day business at a measured pace. Sunday brought an eerie silence to the village. One or two cars crawled up the main street, paused at the right-angled turn for the bridge, then crept quietly to the left in the Clifden direction.

Leaving the bridge behind her, she turned to her right towards a narrow track that shimmied along the banks of the lake. Alicja was a practised hillwalker, having honed her skill on the mountains near her homeland. From an early age she had been told that the most important piece of equipment is a stout pair of boots. With proper footwear, you could go anywhere. She was not very tall, but her diminutive figure worked to her advantage out in the open terrain. She was able to climb with great agility and her regular sessions in the gym and the pool kept her very fit. She was used to marathon walks. Spending an entire day in the countryside was the activity that she liked best of all.

A small white sign with faded black lettering peeped from the bushes. Alicja swept back some brambles and took a photograph. She could barely read the words 'Glann Road 3km'.

The silence was punctuated with the odd riff of an unseen bird. Rhododendrons were beginning to emerge. Below her the lake sparkled. She gathered up her long brown hair and expertly bunched it into a scrunchie. Taking out her mobile phone, she opened the record app and pressed 'start'. For a few minutes she stood still, listen to the lapping of the water and the intermittent birdsong. Then she began to speak.

Day 6: Oughterard, County Galway. I'm on a narrow road – the locals call it a 'boreen' – called the Glann Road. I'm hiking toward the seat of Gráinne Mhaol. She once had a castle in this district. I don't think the ruins remain, but there is a viewing point over the lake dedicated to her memory.

Such a relief to be here – to get away from everything. Alone at last. The next phase of my life can wait. For now, I want to be in tune with the universe on my own terms. Cut off from everything. Isolated.

As she walked, she paused and restarted the recording, sometimes capturing the ambient sounds and at other times adding a spoken comment. She planned to compile a book about her travels, maybe even publish it one day.

She smiled as she remembered the advice she had received from a Norwegian boy who was also backpacking. They had chatted briefly in Eyre Square where people mingled in the open spaces near the train and bus stations. He was returning to Dublin, and she had just arrived in Galway.

'Ramblers' Hostel in Oughterard is cheap,' he told her, 'but it comes at a price.'

She had taken a bus from Galway city to the village and hiked about a kilometre out from the centre. It was almost eight o'clock in the evening when, following the signposts, she turned onto a long driveway. Rounding a bend, she let out a little cry. '*O rany!*' she gasped. What greeted her was an elongated, two-storey building, complete with thatched roof and whitewashed walls, situated beside a man-made lake. The hostel doubled as an angling centre. Rainbow trout broke the surface of the water, shimmering in the gold and white reflection.

Alicja quickly understood what her Norwegian friend meant by 'it comes with a price'. Every resident had to endure an inquisition from the landlady and Alicja was no exception.

Mrs Flaherty had been expecting her before seven o'clock. She greeted Alicja coolly and marched her past the reception up a flight of stairs. She opened a fire door at the top of the stairs and turned right. With a sweep of her hand, the landlady pointed to an open door. 'That's the men's sleeping quarters,' she said, 'Nobody expected tonight.' She bustled towards the next door. 'Here we are, girleen,' she said, and stood back to let Alicja pass.

It was a large room with six bunk beds, three on either side.

'You'll be on your own here tonight. The other ladies headed into the city this afternoon and I'm not expecting anyone else until tomorrow evening. It's quiet at this time of year. Not the best of weather for backpacking just yet.'

Alicja was relieved to hear that she was the only guest.

'Bathroom's here,' said the landlady, indicating the third door – the only door with a key. 'Hot water is off for the night. You can shower in the morning.'

Mrs Flaherty produced an old teacloth from her apron pocket. 'Just giving the place a little dusting,' she said, 'while you settle yourself in.'

Alicja sighed with relief when she removed her backpack. She dropped it onto the nearest bed. The room was sparsely furnished. Aside from the six iron cots which were painted a gaudy green, a tiny dressing table was perched crookedly against the gable-end wall, its mirror stippled with flecks of brown. The walls were covered with tongue-and-groove pine panelling and two small Velux windows suggested the darkening sky outside. Pieces of thatching had lodged around the edges of the windows that had not been opened in some time. Leaves and dirt blocked out most of the daylight. One of the panes was cracked.

The air was musty and even though it was early spring, Alicja could sense that the room had not been heated over the winter. The bedclothes were damp to the touch. A threadbare carpet of indeterminate colour curled up at the edges where it met the walls.

'What's a young lady like yourself doing around these parts?' Mrs Flaherty asked, fixing Alicja with a stare, at the same time pretending to dust the tiny dressing table.

Alicja told her that she was hitchhiking through Europe, taking time off after finishing her degree.

'And what college did you go to?'

'The University of Opole.'

'Where is that?'

Mrs Faherty squinted.

This woman had been pretty once, Alicja thought. Petite, with a slim figure, high cheek bones, and sallow skin. Her hair, once blonde but greying now, was cut in an upside-down bowl shape, and it wobbled like a lump of jelly when she moved. Her eyebrows had all but disappeared. Alicja guessed that she applied pencil liner to resurrect them. She was wearing a frock made of heavy brown material. Around her neck hung a scapular of green twine with a picture of Jesus imprinted on a rectangle of green baize. From time to time she clutched it, pulling it from side to side. Her attire was completed by a striped apron which Alicja thought would be more appropriate for a butcher's shop. The years had not been kind to Mrs Flaherty. When she spoke, she displayed a gap in her upper front teeth. This caused a sharp whistle to accompany her speech.

'Opole? It's in Southern Poland,' Alicja answered. 'Beside the River Oder.'

'You're a bit young for university,' Mrs Flaherty said. 'And what degree was it you got?'

'A medical degree.'

Mrs Flaherty put away the duster into the pocket of her apron. She sat on the edge of the bed.

'A medical degree?' she repeated, letting this nugget clatter around in her inquisitive brain before it finally settled. 'So, you trained to be a nurse?'

A sharp whistle.

'A doctor.'

This produced an expulsion of air and a louder shrill noise.

'A doctor, is it?' The pencil-thin eyebrows raised and knotted. Her eyes narrowed like those of a fox approaching a henhouse. 'Not a suitable job for a girleen, if you ask me...'

Is she implying that I'm from a backward country? Or that women should not be doctors? Surely not!

The landlady pursued her questioning for fully ten minutes. She was no respecter of boundaries. The atmosphere in the room turned decidedly chilly when she turned her attention to boyfriends.

'D'you have a fella?' she asked with a sly grin. She settled her head sideways and her neck disappeared into the bowl of jelly. Alicja looked at the one eye peering up at her: an evil witch offering a poisoned apple to a princess.

'I was just wondering,' continued the witch, 'because it's not often we have a girleen like yourself travelling alone.'

Alicja felt a tightness in her chest. Her jaw ached from clenching her teeth. Uninvited, her thoughts turned to Darek. Darek the romantic. Darek who still had two years to go to become a surgeon. Darek who wanted to sweep her off her feet, marry her and start a family. Their relationship was moving too speedily for her liking. She didn't want her career to be swallowed up by Darek's ambition. Did she really want to settle into married life immediately after qualifying? Yes, she loved him. But she loved life and adventure and travel as well.

'Far be it from me to pry,' said Mrs Flaherty, waiting expectantly for an answer.

Alicja was at a loss for words. She looked at this stranger. The impertinence of you to ask such personal questions. There is a fine line between curiosity and civility.

The landlady's animal instinct sensed the hostility in the air. Just when Alicja thought she could bear it no longer, the interrogation finished as suddenly as it had begun.

'Look at me, sitting on a guest's bed,' said Mrs Flaherty, making a great show of straightening out the creases she had left on the bed spread. 'You must be tired after your journey and me here chattin'. I'm sure you're dying for a nice cup of tea. Will I bring it up to you?'

This change of tone confused Alicja. Her tormentor had morphed into a caring mother figure.

'I'd prefer to have the tea downstairs,' she murmured.

Mrs Flaherty brushed passed her and disappeared down the corridor, saying: 'The kettle will be boiled in five minutes.'

Alicja closed the door and listened to the retreating footsteps. When everything was quiet, she inhaled and exhaled deeply. 'The quicker I get out of here in the morning, the better,' she said to herself as she unpacked her nightclothes from her backpack.

Now she was on this narrow country road which guided her into a plantation of silver birch and conifers, over the Owenriff River and onto an area of open moorland. She was dumbstruck by the remoteness of the place. She made her way to the edge of the lake and sighed with pleasure. Her shoulders dropped, her mind cleared, and she trailed her fingers in the glistening water.

This wilderness area was just what she needed. All thoughts of future work and romantic proposals were banished from her mind. She wanted to stay in the moment.

And there was so much here to command her attention. A lover of nature and of wildflowers, Alicja marvelled at the abundance of native species. Here, she recognised sundew and butterwort, and there, an asphodel. The trail eventually led her onto an old bog road. When planning her route, she had read that this road was rarely used nowadays. In the past, local farmers transported turf or took sheep to and from the mountains along this way. She had read that during the summer, this area was a magnet for hikers with its spectacular panoramic views of Lough Corrib and very little traffic. In fact, the road came to a dead end at a layby near the edge of the lake. Walkers trekked this way for the sheer beauty of the place.

'Follow the trail until you find Gráinne Mhaol's viewing seat,' the guidebook had advised. 'Continue on to the woods. It's possible to camp there.'

Alicja had toyed with the idea of setting up her tent for the night in those woods. The evenings and nights were still chilly in the west of Ireland. She'd wait until later to make up her mind.

The day passed quickly. Alicja went off-trail and explored the newly planted forest and its surrounding bogland. She broke off a small sod of turf and put it into the bottom pocket of her backpack. *A nice souvenir for Mamma.* She spent some time climbing uphill towards the windmills that stood majestically on the higher ground, arms turning, ballerinas performing in the light breezes. Alicja was engrossed in the newness of everything. She busied herself taking notes and making recordings of each fresh discovery. At various intervals she stopped and rested under the warm sun. The idea of setting up camp in the woods was becoming more attractive as the hours passed by.

Just as the sun began to dip towards the surface of the glistening lake, she arrived at the viewing point. Perfect timing. There were two benches, a wooden one on the forest side of the road and a concrete seat on the side facing the lake. A rusty sign confirmed that the one made from stone was Gráinne Mhaol's viewing seat, a site of folklore and legend. It would be an ideal place for Alicja to rest awhile and watch the sunset. A short distance away, a tourist sign displayed a map of the area under the words *Conamara – Fláin go smior* (wild at heart). She laughed when she read the Irish translation for the little note towards the bottom of the sign: *'Watch out for the gardaí. Poitín makers distilled their illicit alcohol on uninhabited islands. The one giveaway to the police was the smoke rising from their turf fires.'*

Had she not walked over to investigate the signpost more closely, she might never have spotted the car partly hidden in a canopy of bushes and trees. It was facing the road, but only a section of the bonnet and the front lights were visible. What caught Alicja's eye was the reflection of the dying sun rays from the silver grille on the front the car.

An abandoned wreck? Her cautious nature battled with her natural curiosity. She raged against the polluters for destroying the beauty of these glorious surroundings. Her indignation caused her to stride towards the car. She pulled back an overhanging branch. What she saw made her freeze in her tracks.

'Policja,' she murmured. The distinctive markings and the bank of blue emergency lights on the roof left her in no doubt that this was a police car. A new car. Not a discarded wreck.

What was it doing in the middle of nowhere?

Where was the policeman?

A crunching sound beneath her feet startled her. Empty beer cans were strewn among discarded cigarette butts next to the driver's door.

Alicja shuddered. All thoughts of rest and watching the beautiful sunset evaporated. She turned on her heels and walked smartly away, back the route she had come. She was puzzled for some time about the presence of that car. *Empty cans? Cigarette butts? A policeman drinking? Dumping rubbish?*

As she put more distance between herself and the car, her trepidation lessened. Her mind became occupied with planning her next move. Would she still have the courage to camp in the woods? Dark clouds had gathered overhead. A small shiver shook her frame. The sky was turning from blue to an ominous black and the first droplets suggested an impending downpour.

Reluctantly, she decided to return to the village. 'There'll be a bed here if you're needing it,' Mrs Flaherty had said kindly. *At this pace, I could be back in Oughterard before it gets completely dark.* She plugged in her earphones. Her music worked its magic and soon she was humming her songs, reflecting with pleasure on her day's achievements.

The last dregs of sunset painted an orange glow in the darkening sky. Alicja caught images of it through the trees as she walked, stopping now and again to trek to the shoreline. From there, she took photographs of the kaleidoscope of colours that streaked over the lake and glimmered on its surface.

The road had many inclines and hollows. Alicja slowed her pace as she crested a small rise. Now, she quickened her stride. She allowed herself to be carried along down the gently sloping incline. Twilight relinquished its grip, and a few errant black clouds chased the last vestiges of sunlight from the sky. The cover of trees drew the curtains on the evening's performance. The weather misbehaved and threw away the rule book, as it often did in the Connemara mountains. The predicted dry evening had given way to a misty rain. Alicja didn't mind. She had come prepared. Stopping in the middle of the track, she removed her yellow, plastic poncho from her knapsack.

A car hurtled over the rise behind her. It gathered speed down the slope. There was a screech of brakes. Alicja was thrown in the air. A blur of yellow came crashing down. When she fell, her neck snapped on a roadside boulder. Alicja's life ended abruptly in the quiet Galway countryside.

A coroner's verdict would state that her injuries were consistent with having been struck by a moving vehicle. The actual cause of death was a broken neck, most likely the result of a fall from a height onto a blunt object, such as a heavy stone. However, this verdict would not be relayed in the immediate aftermath of the accident. A coroner needs a body on the autopsy table to determine cause of death.

The car had come to a halt fifty metres from where Alicja's crumpled body lay. Nobody will know whether Alicja realised what happened to her next. Did she cry out for help? Were her hopes raised by the sound of the approaching footsteps? Was she surprised to hear a person crying? Were those her own cries or someone else's? Did she catch a scent of perfume or aftershave? Did she imagine the smell of nicotine and alcohol? Was she moving now, being dragged and rolled? Did she hear the splash when she entered the freezing ditch water? Did her body shiver? Was her face submerged or did she see the driver hovering over her? Did she hear the footsteps receding, the driver's door opening and closing, and the car speeding off?

Did she scream?

Would anyone look for her?

Who knew where she was going?

Or when she might come back?

She had lost herself in the Irish countryside. Soon, her lifeless body would enter rigor mortis.

By an ironic twist of fate, she had found the isolation she was looking for.

Peppi and the Tuba

To describe him as a purebred, wire-haired fox terrier would be not only a disservice to the breed but an affront to the true essence of his being. Indeed, a considerable portion of fox terrier ran through his veins, but his ancestry was a murky melange of sundry mongrels. His lineage was an enigma, a riddle of genes that defied unravelling. Yet, he was my dog, and I loved him.

Compact and squat, with an inquisitive head, he bore the most singular coat of fur – a wiry amalgamation of stubborn white curls and splatters of brown across his flanks, as if marked by nature's careless paintbrush. From whence the name 'Peppi' sprang, I cannot say. Ultimately, it mattered little, for he never deigned to respond to it.

Daddy had brought him home from the pound on a balmy summer afternoon. 'A dog is not a plaything,' he admonished. 'Someone must take charge of his food and water. And someone will be accountable for cleaning up the mess until he is properly housebroken.'

That someone was me.

My elder brother, Mike, was preoccupied with an ever-shifting cast of girlfriends. My sisters, meanwhile, were immersed in the taxing world of secondary school exams. As for me, I had only just emerged from the confines of primary school, and the vast expanse of a three-month summer hiatus stretched before me like a tantalising promise.

Peppi and I were kindred spirits. His unyielding independence resisted all attempts at domestication. He chose to accompany me on our adventures through the sprawling garden behind our home, and on our Sunday excursions to my uncle's farm.

Peppi was a magnet for mischief. His escapades included infiltrating the chicken enclosure, where my mother had been nurturing a dozen bantam hens. Her complicity in his misdeeds remained a secret between us, shielding him from my father's ire. For several mornings, my father grumbled over the fresh eggs my mother had begun purchasing at the market, but he never pursued the matter further.

In the evenings, when we gathered around the fireplace, Peppi would tenderly lick my mother's toes. Was it an act of gratitude, acknowledging her role in his salvation?

But it was an incident at Uncle Tom's farm that pushed Peppi to the brink of calamity. We were at play in the haggard on a luminous Sunday afternoon when Auntie Josie summoned the children inside for tea. Peppi, however, was beguiled by the sight of four or five felines in the haggard's corner, and no earthly power could deter him from the chase.

All but one of the cats managed to evade him, vaulting over the stone wall to freedom. The hapless straggler sought refuge within a thicket of brambles, its back pressed against the wall, ensnared by the relentless weeds. Peppi's growl reverberated through the air, a war drum's call. Each time he lunged, the cat retaliated, spitting, and tearing at his nose with its talons. Undeterred, Peppi retreated, only to return again and again.

And so it might have concluded, had it not been for the inexplicable impulse that seized me, urging me to defend the honour of my loyal canine companion, who must not be vanquished by a mere feline.

My intent was to embolden him, to urge him on until the cat abandoned its ill-fated post and vaulted over the wall. Alas, events did not unfold as I had envisioned.

'Go on!, Peppi, Go on!,' I exhorted.

He regarded me with an inscrutable expression, and for the first time, chose to obey my command. He thrust his black snout deeper into the brambles, heedless of the lacerating thorns. The cat's claws drew scarlet from his muzzle, and the innate ferocity of the terrier was roused. Driven by a primal surge of testosterone, Peppi pressed forward, like a beleaguered pugilist braving his adversary's onslaught to deliver the decisive blow.

'Stop! Peppi, stop!' I roared. 'Oh, please, stop! Come out, Peppi. Here, boy!'

But it was beyond the point of no return. Peppi had shed his domesticated mantle, and in its stead, the savage beast of the wild reigned supreme. His blood was up. Should I have called my dad? Should I have shouted for help? I glanced down at my shorts, now dampened by my own fear.

Undeterred, the dog clambered on top of the ensnared creature. His teeth pierced soft flesh, and I heard the grisly symphony of splintering bones. Peppi's jaws clamped around the cat's throat, slick with blood—his own or the cat's? The distinction was immaterial. A hush enveloped the haggard, the very birds suspending their breath.

Withdrawn from the brambles, the dog bore his grisly trophy and deposited the lifeless form at my feet.

Inexplicably, Peppi's fortunes remained unscathed. When I ran crying into the farmyard kitchen Mammy took me in her arms. 'There, there, Timmy,' she soothed. 'Let's go up and change those shorts. Daddy and Uncle Tom will sort things outside.'

Upon our return, Tom dismissed the felled creature as a mere stray.

'Worthless in the yard,' he declared. 'Glad to be rid of it.'

In the car on the way home, Daddy just said: 'Let that be a lesson to you. Always keep your dog on a leash when you are near other animals.'

Still snivelling in the back seat, I looked at Peppi. He tenderly licked my nose.

As time went on, Peppi began to behave better, and our family adjusted to his presence. Little did I know that an encounter with a tuba would mark the next chapter in Peppi's story.

It began when mother decided that idle hands were a fertile playground for the devil's machinations. She was determined to keep her children busy during the school holidays. Mike was old enough to work part-time in the bakery. Once a week, Mammy took him to Mrs Connolly for violin lessons. My sisters had a job in the GBC Café helping in the kitchen, collecting dishes, and washing cutlery. On Wednesdays, they got a half day so that they could go to piano lessons with Mrs O'Donnell.

My jobs were to serve at mass twice a week in the Augustinian church and to help Mammy wash up the dishes at home. But that wasn't enough to keep an overactive boy out of devilment!

One Saturday morning, she marched me down the Magdalen Hill towards the Fairgreen.

'I'm not going to work in the abattoir,' I cried. 'I'm not!'

'Don't be foolish, Timmy,' my mother chided. 'You don't think I'd put you working in that stinking place, do you?'

'Oh, Mammy,' I stammered, fighting back the tears. 'I don't want to work on the trains either.'

The train station was accessible through the Fairgreen, and we plodded steadily toward the entrance. Just as we neared it, my mother veered left, leading me up a narrow lane to a stone building that had escaped my notice thus far in my brief existence.

'This is our place!' she declared.

'What's in there, Mammy?'

'Follow me,' she commanded. 'All shall be revealed in due course.'

Inside, a dim passage led to a door at the far end. Without knocking, my mother flung it open, revealing a spacious hall with a stage at the opposite end. A green banner above the stage bore the inscription *St Patrick's Brass Band* in gilded letters.

A cohort of boys marched to and fro across the hall, their steps dictated by the commanding voice of a diminutive, rotund bandmaster.

My mother deposited me into this man's care, with a simple admonition: 'Be well-behaved, Timmy, and heed Mr Lee's instructions.'

Mr Lee swiftly deduced that, while I possessed a robust stature uncommon for my age, my musical aptitude was sorely lacking.

'Even tall, strapping lads have a place among us, young man,' he informed me. 'Let's see how you get on with the drum.'

Two older boys raced to the stage, retrieving a grand crimson drum. They affixed it to me.

'March up and down,' Mr Lee directed.

I managed a mere two strides before collapsing in a heap.

'Unstrap him, boys,' the bandmaster ordered. 'He is not yet ready for that yet. Let's try the bassoon.'

Thus began a succession of trials with an assortment of large brass instruments, culminating in Mr Lee's determination that the tuba and I were destined for one another.

'Now, Timmy, you must learn to march in synchrony with the other lads, maintaining a ramrod-straight back and ensuring the tuba remains upright at all times.'

So began my fleeting, ill-fated dalliance with the art of music. By the third week of practice,

Mr Lee decreed that I should bring the tuba home in order to acquaint myself more intimately with the scales. My task was to purse my lips and exhale through the mouthpiece, manipulating the timbre of the sounds produced. Additionally, I was to learn the pressing of the three valves to generate the notes of a scale.

'Get out into the garden with that yoke,' my father encouraged. 'Don't be making that noise inside of this house.'

I sought refuge in the hen shed. Peppi regarded the gleaming, golden instrument with intense curiosity, tilting his head this way and that as I coaxed a series of discordant tones from the tuba. Upon extracting a particularly shrill note, Peppi endeavoured to mimic the sound with a resonant howl. I continued to blow, spit, and manipulate the valves with reckless abandon, driving the hens from their perches to huddle fearfully in a corner of the shed. I had the sinking feeling that our makeshift orchestra was doomed.

'Mammy,' I implored, 'I don't want to play the tuba. Why can't I get violin lessons like Mike? Or piano lessons?'

'Do you think I'm made of money?' my mother admonished. 'St Patrick's Brass Band is famous, not only here in Galway but all over the world.'

'But Mammy...'

'If you stick with your practice, and you may yet find yourself performing in the St Patrick's Day parade, or perhaps even during the Corpus Christi procession.'

'I've no interest in playing in a parade, Mammy. I don't like the marching. I hate Mr Lee and I don't want the tuba.'

'Very well, Timmy. Go to your practice today, and I'll have a word with Mr Lee later in the week. We'll decide what's best for you.'

'Thank you, Mammy,' I replied. I put my arm around the tuba, opened the front gate and, with a lighter heart, started to walk along the footpath towards the Fairgreen. I had scarcely travelled a short distance when I sensed a presence behind me. Turning, I discovered that Peppi had decided to accompany me.

'Go home, Peppi!' I shouted.

Peppi halted and regarded me with a plaintive expression.

'Go home!' I reiterated, my voice rising in volume. I wheeled about to pursue the recalcitrant dog, who promptly pivoted on his paws and sprinted toward our house.

I resumed my journey, reaching the bottom of Magdalen Hill before hearing a familiar bark emanating from behind me. There was Peppi, head lowered, slinking along in my wake.

Oh, no! I'm already late. What am I to do now? It's much too far to return home!

'Get away, Peppi! Go home, you pup!' Peppi had never been allowed to roam free in the Fairgreen before, and the scent wafting from the abattoir proved irresistible. He bounded toward the source of the enticing aroma.

'Come back!' I shouted, struggling to give chase while burdened by the cumbersome tuba.

Peppi vanished around a corner of the abattoir building.

Where has he gone? Mr Lee will be furious if I'm late again.

As I rounded the corner, I was confronted with a sight that seared itself indelibly into my memory. Peppi had encountered a black cocker spaniel, and the two dogs were engaged in a grotesque, whirling dance. Somehow, their tails had become entwined, binding them together at their rears as they spun about at a dizzying speed.

'Get away!' I shouted at the spaniel. 'Leave Peppi alone!'

The harder the dogs tried to disengage from one another, the more tightly they seemed to be conjoined. I was at a loss for what action to take. Had a stick been within reach, I would have used it to attempt separating the entangled dogs. Unfortunately, I had no stick, but I did have a tuba.

Gripping the instrument by the horn, I hoisted it high above my head, then brought it crashing down upon the backs of the hapless canines. The spaniel emitted a yelp and, suddenly, managed to break free. It fled the scene, whining and limping.

Peppi lay motionless on the ground.

'Oh, Peppi,' I cried. 'What have I done?'

The impact must have struck him on the head.

'I've killed you. My poor, innocent Peppi! Oh, Lord Jesus, pray for the soul of my beloved pet. I'm a murderer, Lord. Take me but save my dear dog.'

Distraught, I knelt beside the lifeless form of my cherished companion. A long strand of red gut protruded from his hindquarters.

'Oh, dear Jesus, I have busted his tummy,' I moaned. 'Oh, my God, I've killed him.'

Furious with the offending instrument, I kicked the tuba aside and gingerly cradled my deceased pet in my arms. 'Peppi, Peppi, if you can hear me, I'm so sorry. I never meant to kill you.'

And, clutching Peppi to my chest, I ran—out of the Fairgreen, up Magdalen Hill—until I reached the gate of my house. All the while, Peppi's gut dangled from his belly, swaying to and fro. Not a spark of life remained in him.

I burst through the back door. 'Mammy, Daddy, I've killed him... I've killed him stone dead.'

'What? What happened, Timmy?' asked Daddy.

'Peppi got stuck with another dog, Daddy. Their tails were locked together. They were going round and round, glued to each other. I had to do something. I used my tuba to separate them. But I killed Peppi. I flattened him. Oh Daddy....'

'There, there, son.... Let me have a look.'

'You see his gut, Daddy? You see his gut sticking out?'

'Yes, son, I see it. Now, you just sit over there, and I'll see what can be done.'

I seated myself at the kitchen table, beneath the portrait of Jesus with his heart in his hands and the red lamp that burned eternally for our immortal souls.

'Dear Jesus, grant me a miracle,' I prayed silently. 'Take me, Lord, for I am a sinner. Let poor Peppi live...'

My father scrutinised the limp body.

'Mam, bring me a basin of cold water,' he said calmly.

Mammy rushed to the sink and filled the basin.

'Stand back,' instructed Daddy.

He upended the basin, dousing the dog in a deluge of water. Miraculously, Peppi sprang to his feet, shook himself vigorously, and appeared bewildered by his surroundings. His gut magically retracted into his tummy, and he looked around in a daze. Catching sight of the open door, he darted into the garden.

'You saved him, Daddy,' I cried. 'You saved him!'

'He was merely stunned, son,' my father explained.

'No, Daddy. He was dead, as Lazarus once was. You're like Jesus, Daddy! It's a miracle.'

'Off you go now, son, and look after your dog.'

I found Peppi frolicking in the grass when I caught up with him. His gut had entirely healed. He playfully nudged an old plastic football with his nose. Peppi was the world's finest goalkeeper. Together, we started a game of penalties.

Some hours later, Mr Lee appeared at our front door, clutching a muddy tuba. Mammy ushered him into the sitting room. For a while, they sat in quiet conversation, punctuated by bursts of laughter. They never summoned me.

I concealed myself behind the stairs as Mammy said goodbye to her visitor and closed the hall door.

'I know you're there, Timmy,' Mammy said. 'Don't worry, child. You don't have to go to band practice any longer. You and Peppi are far safer here at home.'

The Beginning of the End

The pain crept upon him, ascending from his knees to the small of his back, then coursing along his spine, and insinuating itself between his shoulder blades. A cold sweat blossomed through the pores of his skin. An odd tingling sensation, as if some unseen force were at play, began in his fingertips and travelled up his arms. Jack tasted the sour tang of bile rise unbidden in his throat. Struggling to recall the day's lunch, he wondered if some dubious morsel had initiated this sudden bout of nausea. The notion of a heart attack did not even graze his thoughts.

The force, when it struck him, left him utterly winded. He retched, and then the slow-motion tumble started, a dreamlike descent unfurling frame by frame. His boot, instead of finding purchase on a solid rock, caught on a jagged fragment of bogwood, tearing itself free from his foot and sending the remainder of his cumbersome frame off balance. To Jack, it seemed as if the shoreline's rocks rose in a malevolent dance, conspiring to bruise, needle, and batter him. With a fleeting moment of foresight, he maneuvered his plummeting weight so that his left hip and elbow would absorb the brunt of the impact. His left temple met the unyielding stone with a dull, resonant thud.

For a few moments, he lay in abject surrender. Stunned. His consciousness flickered dimly, and he knew, at least, that he was still alive. He willed his toes to move, and they obeyed. Gradually, he took stock of his body, mentally checking his limbs for signs of movement and pain. To his surprise, nothing seemed broken.

Hadn't there been the sound of shattered glass? His spectacles had been flung from his head, surely lying crushed among the seaweed and pebbles. He wasted precious minutes seeking them with his eyes, patting the nearby stones in vain. Then, the realisation dawned that his glasses remained in place upon his head.

'Fool!' he grunted.

Instinctively, he fumbled in his pocket for his mobile phone. Cursing, he felt the shards of broken glass slice into his fingertips. He withdrew his bloodied hand and pressed his fingers to his tongue. The metallic taste made his stomach roil.

For an instant, everything went quiet. Then he heard the swish, swashing of waves and he felt the sea water licking at the legs of his trousers. A brief flash of panic. Better keep calm. Stay in control.

He felt no pain.

There was a certain tranquillity in lying on the rocky shoreline, and his thoughts began to meander.

Five years had passed since he had made his home in Carrickalee. Once, he had been a formidable presence in Dublin—revelling in fat pay cheques, extravagant expenses, entertaining clients, and boozy celebrations. He could carouse with the best of them. But that was another life. In those days, he knew he had the look of a drinker, his face rosy with hints of purple in his cheeks and nose.

But that was then.

Now, he found contentment in the sedate rhythms of life in the foothills of Connemara. A regular at O Máile's, the quayside pub, he would lean against the counter, nursing pints of porter. He drank quietly and often, rarely engaging in extended conversations with anyone. He exchanged pleasantries, commented on the weather, and retreated to his private musings. He made a point of patronising the village's other three pubs as well.

A solitary figure who lived alone, he occasionally mentioned his children, but no visitors ever came to see him.

The end of his marriage had been a slow, drawn-out demise rather than a violent eruption. The separation, when it finally came, took him by surprise. Separation was something that happened to others, not to him.

Until one day, he found her in the living room, weeping. 'We can't go on like this,' she said. 'It'd be better to go our separate ways.'

This argument, or perhaps the one before, had centred on money. Why were they overdrawn again? Why did she need an overdraft? Why was the fridge perpetually stocked with food destined to spoil? Why did she continue catering for children long since flown from the nest? Why were they in debt?

It beggared belief.

Worse still, he found himself unable to broach these matters with her. She had behaved this way her entire life; why should she change now?

He had always cleared her credit card debts, ensured the mortgage was paid, and managed the car repayments.

Water under the bridge, he mused with a wry smile. She would have been furious with him.

'Why do you always speak in clichés?'

'They're not clichés. They're aphorisms.'

'Aphorisms? Clichés? What does it matter? Can't you say anything that isn't an old wives' tale? Or a bon mot? Pardon my French. And before you tell me that I'm mispronouncing, let me tell you that I don't give a flying, French damn! I'm so fed up with your pithy sayings!'

'Excuse me for living!' he shouted.

It was then that she declared they could not continue.

A lump lodged in his throat, refusing to budge, a barrier against the onslaught of raw emotions: anger, guilt, rage, pity. He didn't know what to feel. A schoolboy failing an exam; a grown man failing at marriage. The pain in his gut surged to meet the constriction in his chest.

Gathering his belongings, he purchased a small little place beside the sea—Donnelly's thatched cottage, a seventeenth-century structure recently renovated. The locals knew of the rising damp that plagued the building, but no one bothered to inform Jack. The engineer's report mentioned moist patches but did not emphasise this issue as a reason to avoid purchasing the cottage. Jack's dream home quickly transformed into a cold, humid nightmare. He soon learned that the only way to stave off the persistent moisture was to keep a turf fire burning in the grate, day and night. The

Donnellys had lived long lives; a touch of dampness had not curtailed their existence.

Jack had no choice but to grin and bear it. There was no hope of recouping his investment now.

An improbable friendship blossomed between him and a local fisherman, Fergal Bradley. Fergal loathed everyone in the village, his tongue lashing out with such venom that the locals averted their gaze and shunned his proximity. Yet, somehow, Jack and Fergal found solace in each other's company, a bond formed. It might have been the Labrador that bridged the distance between them. Fergal owned a young Collie pup, and the older Labrador delighted in pursuing the sprightly dog along the shore. Gradually, a conversation unfolded between the two owners, and a companionship took root.

To call it a warm friendship would be an exaggeration. Exchanges about the weather, a remark on the boats in the harbour, and perceptive observations on the tides and seaweed marked their conversations. Jack's interest in the natural world grew, and he posed fresh inquiries to Fergal with each encounter. The two were often found engrossed in profound discussions.

Then, Jack vanished for a time. Went away. If villagers thought of him at all, they assumed he had moved on, never to return.

But Jack reappeared. He had checked himself into rehab as a voluntary patient, and the experience had altered him. The transformation did not go unnoticed.

Subtle changes emerged at first.

'Good morning, Jack! Fine day!'

'No, actually. I find it bitterly cold. The wind would slice through you. In fact, the weather forecast is for rain...'

'Humph! When did you develop an interest in weather forecasts?' a disgruntled villager grumbled, sidestepping Jack, who seemed to stand a few centimetres taller than before.

His visits to the local pubs ceased as well, and he grew more solitary than ever.

A wave doused his face with briny water, jolting Jack back to the present as he lay prostrate on the pebbled shore.

Could I risk trying to rise? He recalled spotting two men strolling along the seashore earlier in his walk. Had they witnessed my fall? Were they within earshot? Keep calm! Keep calm! What if he could not regain his footing? The tide would envelop him. The thought of drowning loomed large. How could he manage to stand without assistance?

Gasping for breath, he fought to suppress the encroaching panic.

One step at a time, he reminded himself. Rome wasn't built in a day. Can I manage to rise to my knees? He maneuvered his body, lying fully on his stomach. A gentle breeze grazed a fresh tear in his trousers just below his left knee. From the stinging sensation, he knew a deep gash bled beneath. His left hand, with fingers already sliced, instinctively reached for the wound. Blood coated his fingers as he drew his hand to his face.

With an anguished groan, he found himself kneeling, the sea water nearly upon him.

Positioned like a panting hound, he mustered all his strength, pushing with his arms while seeking leverage from his right knee. If he were to stumble back into a prone position, he feared he would lack the vigour to repeat this effort. With his remaining strength, he hoisted himself up, taking one or two unsteady steps.

At last, he stood upright, balanced precariously upon the rocks. Blood flowed freely down his left leg. Tentatively, he inched forward, his breathing gradually normalising. After what felt like an eternity, he crossed the short distance to the sandy shoreline, heading directly towards his home. Nobody had noticed. The two men he had seen earlier approached him from behind, continuing their conversation as they passed him. Pride stopped Jack from seeking their assistance. I might have been swept away, and none would be the wiser.

He opened his cottage's garden gate. An odd impulse deterred him from entering. He pivoted and strode back towards the beach. His beloved beach. Reaching the shoreline in a daze, he gazed at the spot of his fall.

How much longer will I be able to wander around independently? His confidence waned, little by little. He no longer felt entirely secure. What if it happens again? I'll soon require company on my walks, and eventually, they will cease altogether.

Jack sensed the beginning of the end and shuddered at the thought. The fading light of the setting sun cast elongated shadows across the rocky shore. Amidst the shimmering shards of glass, a small, brown object caught his eye. More purposeful now, he navigated the pebbles and rocks towards the site of his tumble. His blood-filled boot remained lodged in the jagged bog oak, while fragments of his shattered mobile phone lay scattered about.

How can this be?

He stared, perplexed, at his bare feet. The waves ebbed and flowed. Bloodied water swirled around his toes, lapping at his shins. He looked out to sea, where a mysterious shape bobbed amidst the waves, obscured by seaweed. Gingerly, Jack picked his way over stones and pebbles, venturing into the swell for a closer inspection. He waded onward until the ground vanished beneath him.

Once he reached the enigmatic bundle, he knew he would be finally at peace.

Acknowledgements

Frank Fahy wishes to thank Galway County Council for funding towards this project.

All monies from royalties, sales, and other promotions go into the Write-on coffers to help fund future publications and other literary activities.

Comhairle Chontae na Gaillimhe
Galway County Council

'We are all apprentices in a craft where no one ever becomes a master.'

Ernest Hemingway, *The Wild Years*

Printed in Poland
by Amazon Fulfillment
Poland Sp. z o.o., Wrocław

20628714R00125